DANNY ORLIS

AND THE

HEADSTRONG LINDA PENNER

DANNY ORLIS

AND THE

HEADSTRONG LINDA PENNER

BERNARD PALMER

Danny Orlis and the Headstrong Linda Penner
© 2024 by Bernard Palmer
All rights reserved. First edition 1963.
Second edition 2024.

Cover image: Adobe Firefly
Character illustrations: John Ball
Editor: Jon D. Fogdall

Aneko Press Youth

www.anekopress.com

Aneko Press, Life Sentence Publishing, and our logos are trademarks of Life Sentence Publishing, Inc.
203 E. Birch Street
P.O. Box 652
Abbotsford, WI 54405

JUVENILE FICTION / Religious / Christian / Action & Adventure

Paperback ISBN: 979-8-88936-010-0

eBook ISBN: 979-8-88936-011-7

10   9   8   7   6   5   4   3   2   1

Available where books are sold

CONTENTS

CHAPTER 1

BOY CRAZY

It was a warm Sunday afternoon in northern Minnesota. Although it was still winter, the sun had come out while Danny and Kay were in church and had begun to melt the snow a little. When dinner was over Danny suggested that they go for a ride.

"I left my briefcase in the plane at the airport yesterday," he explained. "I thought we could go after it."

Kay took her coat from the hall closet. "That sounds like an excuse to me."

"Who would need an excuse on a nice afternoon like this?"

They drove through the business district, past the church, and across town to the park that slept peacefully under a heavy blanket of snow.

"I'm certainly glad Boyd Patterson isn't working over at the station on Sundays," Danny said.

"He's really been growing in the Lord since he got saved."

"I think we have the Bible club to thank for that. Studying with the other kids has been a strengthening thing for all of them."

"I don't think it's done much for Linda Penner," Kay added.

Her youthful husband nodded. "I'll have to agree with you on that, but what made you think of her all of a sudden?"

"She's over there on the street corner talking to that Olson boy." Disappointment edged her voice.

Danny glanced in the direction Kay was pointing. "I think you're getting excited over nothing, Kay. She's got her little sister, Becky, with her, and all they're doing is standing there talking. They're not doing anything out of the way that I can see."

She laid a hand on his arm.

"I know I sound terribly nosy, Danny, but I've got reason to believe Linda's meeting that boy behind her dad's back."

"Now wait a minute. Just because they're talking on the street corner is no sign that they're even going together."

"I've seen her with this same boy five or six times in the past two or three weeks. They're always on a street corner, or in a drugstore, or getting into his car together."

"Did it ever occur to you that they could be good friends?"

"Look at them, Danny. He's holding her hand now. And see how she looks up at him. She thinks she's really and truly in love with him." There was a short pause. "And that's not all that bothers me. She's not even old enough to be dating. I'm sure she's not a day over fourteen. And that Olson boy is as old as Ron unless I'm badly mistaken. He must be twenty-one or so. That sort of thing can only lead to trouble."

Even as they watched, Linda Penner threw back her head and laughed.

"Want to break this meeting up, Kay?" Danny asked. Without waiting for her answer, he made a U-turn and pulled over to the curb near Linda and Becky.

Kay rolled down the window. "Hello, Linda," she called.

The girl's eyes brightened. "Hello, Mrs. Orlis."

"You girls look cold. Would you like a ride home?"

There was an instant's hesitation. Linda glanced down at Becky. "I'm not very cold. Are you, Becky?"

The young man who had been talking to Linda broke in quickly. "I've got my car over there. I'll take the girls home."

Danny Orlis opened the car door and got out. "I think your dad would like it better if you come with us, Linda." He spoke kindly enough, but there was no mistaking the steel in his voice.

"I suppose that's right." She turned to the Olson boy. "I'm sorry, but I've got to be going. I'll be seeing you."

Maynard Olson took hold of her arm and held it for a moment. "I'll call you tomorrow night, Linda."

She turned quickly, fear burning in her eyes. "Oh, don't do that," she retorted in a voice she thought would not carry. "Dad might be home. I–I'll call you."

"I'll be waiting for you to call. Don't disappoint me."

Linda followed Becky into the back seat of the car. "I don't think it's so cold that we have to have a ride home," she pouted. "We could just as well have walked."

Danny laughed. "I suppose it wouldn't have hurt you any, but it would be foolish to walk when we can take you right to your front door."

There was a short, strained silence. Finally, Kay Orlis turned and leaned on the back of the seat. "Linda," she asked quietly, "does your father know about Maynard?"

The girl's dark eyes blazed. "Does he know *what* about him?" she demanded testily.

"Does he know that you are meeting Maynard Olson on the street?"

The girl's cheeks tinged with red. "There's nothing wrong with talking to–to an old friend on the street. And that's all Maynard is. He's just a friend of mine. We happened to meet and talk for a little while this afternoon, that's all."

Kay chose her words carefully. "I know you're thinking that I'm getting out of order talking with you like this, Linda, but don't you think Maynard is awfully old for you? He's half again as old as you are. He's probably been out of high school for three or four years."

"I don't see what that's got to do with it," the girl countered. "We aren't going together or anything like that. So, you don't need to get so shook up about it."

They stopped at the Penner home and the girls got out. Becky's smile was mischievous and friendly. Linda thanked them, but with some reluctance.

When Danny and Kay were alone in the car once more, he turned to her. "Well, you've had your little talk with Linda, but I don't think you got through to her." He turned toward the airport. "I'm afraid Mr. Penner is going to have his hands full with that young lady."

Kay nodded. "And it's going to get much worse before it gets better."

Danny got his briefcase from the mission plane and drove back to town. "The worst of it is," he said, "Linda is a very attractive girl, and looks quite a little older than she actually is. The boys are going to start ringing her phone any day now."

"From the way it looks they've already started."

They stopped in the drive beside their home and went inside.

"Danny," Kay questioned suddenly, "do you think we should talk with Mr. Penner about this?"

He hung up his coat thoughtfully.

"I just don't know. I'd want to think about it and pray about it before I said anything to him to be sure we're doing the Lord's will. Actually, we don't know very much yet. What we saw today could have been perfectly harmless. And if it is, we'd be doing Linda an injustice by running to her parents."

Kay switched on the floor lamp and sat down in an easy chair nearby. "I know that," she replied. "But we don't want to wait until the problem is a big one before we talk to Mr. Penner. That won't be helping Linda."

Danny perched on the arm of her chair and put his hand on her shoulder. "No, that's true. But we have to be sure."

When Danny and Kay went to church that evening, Linda and Becky were there with their dad. When chubby eight-year-old Becky saw Kay standing alone in the church foyer, a smile broke across her dimpled face, and she squealed with delight.

"Oh, Daddy," she exclaimed, "there are Mr. and Mrs. Orlis. You remember, I told you that they brought Linda and me home this afternoon." She waved gaily. "Hi."

With that Becky broke away from her dad and went running to Kay. She put her arm about the Orlis girl's waist and squeezed her affectionately.

Kay returned her hug. "How are you, Honey?" she asked.

Becky Penner turned her soft brown eyes up to Kay adoringly. "Can I sit with you and Mr. Orlis?" Her voice was appealing. "Can I?"

Kay's answering smile was warm and friendly, and it must have whispered to Becky that she had already made room for her in her heart. "Of course, you may sit with us, my dear," she answered her, "if your daddy doesn't care. We'd love to have you."

The younger Penner girl pulled away from Kay's embrace. "I'll go and ask him if I can sit with you," she said, "but I know he won't care."

Danny smiled down at her as she went scampering away. In a moment she was back.

"See, he didn't care. I just knew he wouldn't."

Danny followed Kay and Becky down the aisle to the pew where they usually sat. The light-haired girl squeezed as close to Kay as she could and took her hand possessively.

Danny Orlis reached over and tangled his fingers in her hair. She glanced in his direction and impishly wrinkled her nose at him.

"I like you," her eyes told him.

After the service Henry Penner came over to Danny and Kay immediately. "I thought I'd better come over and claim my daughter."

"You don't have to claim her if you don't want to, Henry," Danny told him good-naturedly. "We'll be glad to take her home with us."

A strange look crossed Henry's face but faded as he smiled. "I want to thank you for giving the girls a ride home this afternoon." He paused and directed his attention to Kay. "Becky seems quite taken with you, Mrs. Orlis."

Kay drew the little girl closer under her arm and hugged her. "I'm the one who's been taken with Becky, Henry. She's a lovely little girl."

Mr. Penner smiled sadly. "Becky still misses her mother a great deal." He turned and spoke softly to Danny, so the girl would not hear. "I've tried to give Becky and Linda love enough to make up for that which they should be getting from their mother, but I'm afraid I don't do a very good job of it."

"They're two very sweet girls," Danny told him.

Danny and Henry Penner visited for a few minutes. After a time, Mr. Penner drew Danny to one side where they could talk in private.

"I've got a little problem coming up, Danny," he said, "and I've been wanting to talk with someone about it but haven't been able to."

"I'll be glad to talk with you any time, Henry. Just give me a ring so you'll be sure I'm home."

"Thanks. I'll be stopping at your house one of these nights."

Before they left Becky put her arm about Kay's waist once more and squeezed her lovingly. "Can I sit with you in church next Sunday, Mrs. Orlis?" the little girl asked.

"Oh, I'd love that."

Jim Morgan came up just then and the three of them left the church together. Danny turned to his young wife.

"It looks as though you've got yourself a new friend, Kay."

Kay's fingers tightened impulsively on Danny's arm. "She's just about the sweetest, most adorable little friend anyone could have."

Danny opened the car door for Kay. "She's a real cutie," he agreed. "I'd like to steal her and run away with her."

Kay Orlis stopped momentarily on the sidewalk just outside the car. "I feel so sorry for her I can hardly stand it. The poor little tyke misses her mother so much. That's why she clung to me the way she did."

Danny closed the door behind her, went around to the other side, and got in.

"Poor Henry," he sighed. "I'm afraid he's got his work cut out for him."

CHAPTER 2

A FATHER'S DILEMMA

The following afternoon when Danny Orlis got home from the airport Boyd Patterson was waiting in the living room to talk to him.

"Hi, Boyd," Danny greeted him, "how're things going?"

Boyd grinned sheepishly. "Everything's going fine – or at least they would be if I could come up with a couple of handfuls of A's right quick."

Danny crossed the room and sat down. "From the sound of that I take it that you've got some grade trouble."

"Trouble's no name for it. To tell you the truth, Danny, I'm into it clear up to my ears. It's a lot deeper than that, even. It's just about to drown me."

The young pilot paused. "Anything we can do to help?" he asked.

Boyd's eyes lighted hopefully. "Would you, Danny? Would you?"

"I can't promise too much myself," Danny explained, "because I'm gone so much. But I'm sure Kay will be glad to help you when I'm not in. To tell you the truth, you may want her all the time. She was a lot better in the grade department than I ever was, anyway."

"That'd be great. The coach promised me I could go out for baseball this spring if I get my grades up. But I goofed off before I was saved and now, I'm beginning to pay for it."

Danny nodded. "That's the way it goes. That brings up a question, Boyd. How're things going with you spiritually?"

The boy's smile grew wider and wider. "Wonderful!" he exclaimed, his eyes lighting. "Accepting Christ as my Savior is the most wonderful thing I ever did."

* * *

Danny Orlis had half expected Henry Penner to come over to the house to see him early in the week, but it was not until Friday night that he appeared. He entered the modest Orlis home uneasily and, in response to Danny's invitation, sat down on a living room chair.

Danny Orlis pulled up a chair across from him. "It's certainly good to see you, Henry. How've you been?"

The tall, raw-boned visitor turned his cap nervously with calloused hands. For a moment or two the silence was strained and awkward. "I've been meaning to get here sooner, but you know how it goes sometimes. I've had a lot of work to do at the house after I got home from the job."

He paused, fumbling for words, and Danny nodded understandingly. "I suppose it's silly for me to come over and bother you with my troubles, Danny," he began again. "I know you've got plenty of troubles of your own. But you and your wife seemed so interested in the girls and–and I've got to have someone to talk to."

Kay came into the room quietly and sat down just inside the door. Danny and their distraught visitor scarcely noticed her.

"I don't know whether we'll be able to help you much, Henry," Danny said, "but we're certainly happy to listen and pray with you."

He took a deep breath. "I suppose you knew that my wife died unexpectedly a couple of years ago."

Kay Orlis nodded in sympathy. "The pastor's wife told us."

Henry Penner shifted his position uneasily. "Linda and I've been trying to keep things going at home ever since. And, if I do say so myself, she's done a good job of keeping the house clean and looking after Becky."

"That is a big job for a girl Linda's age. It must be awfully hard for her."

"I'm beginning to see that more and more," Henry went on. "She can do the work, all right, but she's still only a little girl and needs supervision and guidance herself."

Danny Orlis leaned forward. "And one of the bad things about that," he agreed, "is that the situation is going to get worse in the years just ahead. The older Becky gets the more supervision she's going to have to have. And I suppose that'll be true of Linda, too."

Henry Penner sighed deeply. "Don't think I haven't lain awake a good many nights thinking about that. I've been thinking perhaps my sister could come and stay with us, but she isn't too well, and has her own family to look after. And even if I could find someone who could come and keep house for us, I wouldn't have too much money to pay her."

"I know just what you mean."

The corners of Henry Penner's mouth twitched nervously.

"I've only told you part of the trouble I'm facing, Danny. The dairy I drive for is opening a fine new route and I'm in line for it."

"That sounds great. It's an advancement, I suppose."

"It can amount to that," Henry went on, "but it'll take time. The route will have to be built up first."

"I see."

"I'd like to have it, though, because I think it can be built up into a very good thing."

"We'll certainly be praying that you get it."

"It's not quite as easy as it sounds," Henry went on. "If I do take it, I'll be home late two nights a week and two nights I'll have to be away from home."

Kay looked at him quickly. "That would mean that

Linda and Becky would be completely unsupervised for much of the time."

The girls' father nodded. "That's the thing that has me so disturbed. Linda hasn't taken a stand for Christ, and she's gotten so interested in boys all of a sudden that I'm very concerned about her." He looked from one to the other. "I just don't know what to do!"

For a long while Danny sat there, looking at Henry. Trouble lined the older man's angular face.

"We'll certainly be praying for you, Henry," Danny said after a time, "and for the girls, too. I know what a burden this is for you."

His guest smiled briefly. "Thanks, Danny." "He arose to go. "I shouldn't be over here burdening you with my troubles. You've got plenty of things on your minds without bothering with me."

Danny got to his feet and took a step or two in the direction of their guest. "Now, Henry," he reminded him, "we want you to feel free to come over and talk with us any time. You've got a serious problem. We want to help you in any way that we can."

"Don't think I don't appreciate it," he answered. "It wouldn't be quite so bad if the girls were a little older, or if I had someone here in town to look after them. But as it is, if I'm not home, there's no one to take care of them."

As he talked, he moved toward the door and Danny walked with him, his arm draped over Henry's shoulder. "You need a lesson from my dad, Henry," he said, "just as I do every once in a while. When I get disturbed about something and don't know what to do or which way to turn, he always reminds me that I should take it to the Lord and leave it there."

Henry Penner's face relaxed a little. "Well, he's certainly right about that, but it's one of those things that is easier to talk about than it is to do."

Henry left and Danny closed the door behind him. For a long minute he stood there thinking.

Kay came over to him. "The poor man," she said softly.

Danny turned. "He's got a real problem. There's no getting around that." He went over to the sofa and sat down, thoughtfully scratching his chin with his thumbnail.

"I'd like to be able to help him," he continued, "but I sure don't know what I could do." Slowly he turned to face Kay. "What do you tell a guy who's got a problem so big there doesn't seem to be any way around it?"

Kay smiled teasingly. "What did you tell Henry about taking it to the Lord and leaving it there?"

Danny was silent for a moment or two. "I might've known you'd come up with that," he told her. "Actually, that's the only thing we can do with a problem like this, and the best thing we can do with any problem."

Kay moved quietly to the sofa and sat down beside him. Her eyes reflected her deep concern. "I know that Mr. Penner has a real problem in getting someone to stay with his girls, and that's probably bothering him more than anything else right now, but I'm afraid he has an even bigger problem than that."

"Linda?"

She nodded seriously. "I don't know why I'm so terribly concerned about her," she went on. "I suppose it's because I remember what it was like when I was her age and was tempted to do some of the same things she's tempted to do. But, Danny, I can't get her out of my mind."

He uncrossed his legs and sat up straight. "She reminds me of the way Roxie used to be," he said. "Of course, Roxie knew Christ as her Savior, but there was a long time after she and Ron first went to high school in Cedarton that she was so anxious to be popular and have boyfriends that she was doing most of the things the unsaved kids were doing."

"That's right. I'd forgotten all about that." She leaned over and picked an imaginary piece of lint off Danny's jacket. "Linda hasn't made a decision for Christ, though, and that has made her problem all the more difficult." She paused briefly. "I can't quite understand why I feel so drawn to Linda. She's actually not a very likeable child."

A smile came to Danny Orlis' eyes. "Becky is the one who's appealing to me. That little gal has a way of wrapping her arms right around your heart."

Kay's smile came back again. "Becky is a darling, and she misses her mother so very much. But Linda is sweet, too. I shouldn't have said what I did a minute ago. She has a lot of wonderful qualities and is doing more than anyone has any right to ask a girl to do in trying to take care of a house and a younger sister and go to school." There was a moment's hesitation. "If she would only take Christ as her Savior and consecrate her life to Him."

* * *

The following evening Boyd Patterson came over to get Kay Orlis to help him with his algebra. Danny had come home from the airport a short time before and was reading the paper in the living room when the student came in.

He looked up. "Hi, Boyd, how's the studying now? Are you beginning to get those grades up?"

"They aren't up where they should be yet, but they're coming now. Especially since Kay started to help me. She's a whiz!"

Danny laid the paper aside momentarily. "I'm glad to hear that."

"You know, Danny," Boyd continued, "I think I'm going to be able to get my grades up soon enough so I'll be eligible for baseball this spring. That's what I'm workin' on."

"I'm glad to hear that, Boyd. And once you get them up it'll be a lot easier to keep them there."

"You can say that again. There's no excuse for a guy to let his grades go the way I did." Boyd started for the kitchen door but turned back with an afterthought. "Now, if I just had my driver's license back again so I could drive, everything would be just about perfect." He pulled out a chair and sat down at the kitchen table.

Kay sat down beside him. "Where do we start this evening, Boyd?" she asked him.

He ran his fingers through his hair and grinned at her sheepishly. "It's algebra again, Mrs. Orlis. I don't think I can ever master it."

"You're coming along fine."

"The trouble is that every time I learn one thing, I find out there's six other things I've got to know, too," he sighed deeply. "I'm afraid algebra's going to be the ruination of me."

"You do as Kay says," Danny called out, "and she'll make you into a regular Einstein!"

CHAPTER 3

JUST WHAT CAN BE DONE?

A day or so later Danny Orlis met Henry Penner in the post office and talked with him. Henry was relaxed and smiling.

"It looks as though God has really answered our prayers, Danny," he said. "I got a letter from my sister yesterday. She's found someone to keep house for us."

"That's great. I'm sure that was a big relief for you."

"You can say that again."

"And I suppose you're taking the new job?"

They walked over to one of the big outside windows together and stood looking out over the street.

"This Mrs. Johnson is going to be coming so she can start work Monday morning." Henry replied. "I'll be taking over the new route then."

Before they parted Danny invited Henry and the girls over for dinner on Saturday evening.

Saturday morning Kay and Danny got two chickens

at the grocery store near their home, and when their guests arrived that evening dinner was practically ready. Becky Penner came running to Kay as soon as she saw her and threw her arms about her waist.

"Oh, Kay," she exclaimed, "I've been so awfully lonesome for you."

Kay Orlis held her tightly. "I've been lonely for you, too, Becky."

Danny Orlis came over and tangled his fingers in her hair. "Hi there, Small Fry, aren't you going to say 'hello' to me, too?"

She turned to him, her tender young face looking up at him. She released herself slowly from Kay's embrace and went to Danny. "I'm glad to see you, too, Uncle Danny."

"You'd better be." He leaned down beside her and swept her into his arms. "You'd just better be."

Fourteen-year-old Linda Penner stood to one side, self-consciously, a slight sneer lingering on her lips. "Hello." She spoke uncertainly.

Kay went over to her, smiling warmly, and took her youthful hand in both of hers. "We're so glad you could come, Linda."

The girl hesitated. For a brief moment she acted as though she wanted to respond to Kay's overtures of friendship but wasn't quite sure just how to go about it, or how she would be received.

"I didn't want to come," she finally blurted, her lips curling about the words, "but Daddy made me."

Kay continued to talk as though she had not heard what Linda said.

Danny Orlis saw that Henry Penner was strangely quiet at the dinner table, but it was not until they had finished eating and had gone to the living room to sit down that he began to talk.

"I just got quite a jolt, Danny," he said suddenly. "You know that Mrs. Johnson who was coming to take care of the girls?"

The young pilot nodded. "She's due in here tonight on the eleven o'clock train, isn't she?" he asked.

"She was due in here tonight," Henry corrected. "In fact, she called me this morning and asked if I would meet her at the train. But just a little while before we were to come over here, I got a wire from her. Her daughter took ill suddenly and was taken to the hospital. Mrs. Johnson's not going to be able to come after all." The hurt stood full in his eyes.

"That's too bad, Henry," Danny said. "How long will she be delayed?"

"It's not a delay. The way I understood the wire she won't be able to come at all." He paused, took a deep breath, and sighed slowly.

"I suppose now you won't be able to take the new job for a while, will you, Henry?"

"That's what makes things even worse. I've already given up my old job, and they've hired a man to take my place. If I don't take the new route, I'll just be out of work."

"Couldn't this new man take over for you on the new route so you could go back to the job you've been on?" Danny wanted to know.

Henry shook his head. "This new route takes a man with considerable experience," he said. Hopelessness flickered in his somber eyes. "If I don't take the new job, I'll be out. I won't have work at all!"

For the space of two or three minutes no one was able to say a word. Danny eyed Henry sympathetically.

"That is tough," he managed. "I wish there was something I could say to help – something I could do."

Desperation gleamed in his companion's eyes. "I don't think there's anything that anyone can do." His voice faltered. "I've never been in a spot like this before." He ran a big hand across his face and through his graying hair. "There just isn't any way out, Danny. I can't leave the girls at home alone, even though it costs me my job. That's for sure." His throat tightened and he swallowed hard. "I've had to leave them far too much the way it's been. But I've got to have work, Danny. I've got some bills that have to be paid and very little in the way of savings." He got to his feet and paced across the floor and back. "I–I tell you I just don't know what to do."

Danny's gaze met Kay's, questioningly.

She was the first to speak. "I haven't talked this over with Danny, Henry," she said, "but I'm sure that he's thinking the same thing that I am. We'd be glad to take the girls into our home and look after them until you're able to find another housekeeper."

Their guest replied quickly. "Oh no, I won't have that. I couldn't presume on your friendship in that way. I–I'll manage somehow."

Smiling broadly, Danny then spoke up. "I think that's a wonderful idea, Kay. Henry, it would be great to have your youngsters with us until you could get someone to take over in your home."

"I wouldn't think of that, Danny. I couldn't take advantage of our friendship by asking you to do something like that."

"You wouldn't be taking advantage of us, Old Man. We'd love to have them, wouldn't we, Kay?"

"Of course we would. You should hear Danny rave about Becky, Mr. Penner. He thinks she's about the cutest, most delightful little girl he's ever seen."

"We really want to take them, Henry," Danny urged. "I mean it. If you have any trouble with us, it'll be in trying to get them back."

There was a short silence before Kay Orlis turned to their distraught guest. "Henry," she began, "did it ever occur to you that perhaps this may be God's answer to your prayers and to ours? We've been praying with you that God would help you to provide for the girls. This could be the way He is providing."

Henry Penner was a long while in answering.

"I'd never thought of it quite that way," he admitted, turning the matter over in his mind. "That does make a difference – a very big difference. And I do need someone to care for the girls."

Linda Penner, who had just come in from taking Becky for a walk, stepped up to her father. "Daddy," she exploded, "I heard what you said just now. You talk as though I'm just a child. I can take care of myself and Becky. You don't have to have anyone to stay with us. We'll get along all right by ourselves. We always have."

Kay's smile was appealing. "What's the matter, Linda?" she asked quietly. "Don't you want to stay with us?"

The girl responded slightly. She smiled in return, and some of the scorn went out of her face. "It isn't that. I think it would be nice staying with you and Mr. Orlis. But Daddy insists on treating me as though I were a baby. I don't have to have anyone to take care of myself."

Danny then turned to her. "You've done well with Becky, Linda," he commended her. "Kay and I have often remarked what a good job you've done in taking care of her the way you have. But a job like that is too big for a girl of your age. And I'm sure you'd like to have someone like Kay to help you with your homework and give you advice when you've got some problem that seems to be too big for you."

"I–I suppose it would be all right." She spoke reluctantly. "But I sure don't want anyone bossing me around."

Danny and Kay acted as though they had not heard what she said. If Mr. Penner noticed her remark, he gave no sign.

His voice trembled with emotion. "I know this must be of God," he faltered. "Why else would I have talked with you about this problem? The pastor is the only other person I have even mentioned it to." He paused momentarily. "And why would you have invited us over here this evening? You've never entertained us before."

"I feel the same way, Henry," Danny agreed. "God often uses circumstances to show us His guidance and will for our lives."

Much of the concern had fled from their visitor's eyes. "I want you both to know that I'm very grateful for what you're doing. I'm sure the girls won't have to stay with you for more than a week or two. I'll advertise for another housekeeper Monday, and I should have someone before very long."

Danny and Kay Orlis were so excited that night they had difficulty getting to sleep.

"It's going to be so nice to have the girls with us, Danny," Kay told him, "even though it's only going to be for a few days. Those youngsters are so sweet, and they do need someone to look after them."

Danny laughed. "It is going to be great having them around for a while."

"You know," his young wife said thoughtfully, "we may be able to do something for Linda spiritually while she's with us."

"I was just thinking the same thing. We'll have to pray a lot about that."

The following morning at the breakfast table Danny told Jim Morgan that Linda and Becky Penner would be staying with them for a while.

"It'll be great to have Becky around," Jim said. "She's cute."

"Most of the guys think Linda's sort of cute, too," Danny told him.

"Cute?" Jim echoed in disgust. "Her?"

"You can't kid me. You know she's cute. I've seen you watching her during our Bible club."

"Only because she's always makin' such a fool of herself," he countered. "You should see the way she runs after the guys at school, Danny. It's enough to make you sick."

"Come off it," Danny laughed. "You just don't want us to know how much you like her."

"Aw, Danny. For cryin' out loud, don't tease me about her. I'm givin' it to you straight. If you think I'm spreading it on, just ask any of the guys at school. You'll find out. She chased after Boyd for a while. Then she started chasin' after one of the other guys on the basketball team. Everybody at school is onto her by now. They duck when she starts in their direction."

"We'll see. We'll see."

Jim Morgan was silent for a moment or two, studying his plate thoughtfully. When he looked up determination steeled his face. "It's swell that the girls are going to be able to stay with us, Danny," he said. "It was pigheaded of me to start spoutin' off about

Linda. I–I'm glad you're going to be able to help her and Becky. But, Danny, I can tell you this much right now. Linda Penner's going to have to leave me alone. That's all there is to it."

Kay Orlis, who had been listening in silence, began to smile. "I just wonder," she observed quietly, "if girls who act the way Linda has been acting around boys actually realize that most guys feel the way Jim does about being chased."

"If they did," Jim said, "they wouldn't do it anymore. And that's for sure."

* * *

Early Monday morning, before Henry Penner left town to take over the new milk route, he drove to the Orlis home with a couple of suitcases and an armload of dresses. "I've got some of the girls' things here, Kay," he said. "This should be enough to last them until I get back. I'll get the rest of their things over to you a little later in the week."

Kay had him put the bags in the front bedroom.

"Thank you, Kay," he said fervently. "I'll never be able to repay you for the way you and Danny are helping us. I don't know which way I could have turned for help if it hadn't been for you."

"We're the ones who should be thanking you," she said. "We're going to enjoy having the girls with us."

Linda and Becky went directly to school from

their home that morning and it was not until late that afternoon that they arrived at Danny and Kay's. Boyd Patterson had stopped by again and was sitting at the kitchen table with Kay when Linda came in. Her eyes brightened as she saw him, and the pout left her lips.

"Well, hello, Boyd," she chirped, "I didn't expect to see you over here this afternoon."

He looked up and grunted at her. "I'm still having some trouble with these new equations, Kay. I thought I had them until we had a pop quiz this afternoon. I'm afraid I flunked it miserably."

Linda Penner pulled up a chair beside Boyd. "Are you going to be able to play baseball this spring, Boyd?" she asked. "I sure hope so. It won't even seem like it's the same if you aren't pitching."

"I've got to get this algebra up or I won't even be able to play," he told her.

"I was talking to some of the kids today," she said, her voice rising indignantly, "and I told them I thought the teachers were just picking on you. I know some of the kids don't study half as hard as you do, and they still get twice as good grades. I don't think there's anything fair about it."

Boyd Patterson turned his attention to the book once more and did not answer her.

"I sure wish I knew algebra," she went on. "I'd help you get your grades up."

Boyd started to speak sharply but glanced up at Kay and stopped.

"Linda." Kay spoke softly, but her voice was firm. "I think you had better go into the other room so Boyd can study. He doesn't have much time."

The dark-haired girl did not move. She stopped speaking, but that was the only sign that she had even heard what Kay had said to her.

"Linda."

"Go right ahead," Linda retorted. "I won't bother any. I'll just sit here."

Kay's eyes met hers, forcefully.

"I want you to go and leave us alone, Linda. We have a great deal of studying to do and it isn't fair to Boyd for you to bother him."

"I won't bother him."

"Linda!" Her voice rose sharply. She pushed back her chair and stood. "I told you to leave the room and that's what I mean. I can't have you disobeying me."

For a brief instant their eyes met and fought silently.

CHAPTER 4

REAL EMBARRASSMENT

anny Orlis, who had overheard the strong exchange of words between his wife and Linda Penner, came into the kitchen quickly. His lips were thin and firm. "Linda." Danny spoke gently, but with a stern tone that could not be ignored. "You heard Kay ask you to go into the other room so she and Boyd wouldn't be disturbed. I think you had better do as she asked you to."

In the silence that followed Boyd Patterson looked nervously to his books. Danny did not move nor speak again.

Flushing scarlet, Linda pushed back from the table and leaped to her feet. For a brief instant her blazing eyes met Danny's and held there defiantly. Then her will seemed to break. She pushed by Danny and went running to her bedroom. The door slammed loudly behind her.

For the space of half a minute or so no one spoke. Then Boyd cleared his throat.

"You know, Danny," he said, "that sounded just like it used to sound around our house. Before I was saved, I used to talk to my parents that way. I sure didn't realize how terrible it sounded."

"Or how terrible it is," Danny answered. "You know, the Bible tells us to honor our father and our mother. We're not Linda's parents, of course, but I'm afraid she talks to her dad the same way she talked to Kay just now."

"That's the way I used to be, that's for sure," Boyd admitted. "The most wonderful thing that ever happened to me was when I took Christ as my Savior and first began to see all the things that were wrong with my life." He grinned crookedly. "If we could just make the other kids at school realize how good it is to be a Christian, they'd all be saved. Satan sure has got them fooled."

Kay Orlis helped Boyd with his studies for an hour or more, with the result that dinner was later than usual that evening. When she finally had the meal ready, Linda was still in her room, the door tightly closed.

Kay turned to Becky Penner. "We're about ready to eat now, Becky. Would you please call Linda?"

Becky's young face puckered impishly. "I can call her, Auntie Kay, but it won't do any good. She's awfully mad at everybody. She says she's not going to eat anything tonight."

Kay looked up at Danny hesitantly. "What should I do, Danny? Do you think I should go in and talk with her?"

"I wouldn't do anything except call her to dinner," he replied. "It might be all right for you to call her rather than sending Becky, but that's as far as I'd go."

"I think I would feel a little better calling her myself. After all, this is the first day with us. I hate to get started out wrong."

In a moment or two Kay was back. "I called her, but I don't know whether it did any good or not. She wouldn't say whether she was going to come and eat."

Danny lowered his voice. "I've got a hunch that this is a little trick of hers to find out just what we're going to be like. I think she wants to find out if we're soft or hard."

Jim Morgan came in and they sat down at the table. They had scarcely finished asking the blessing when Linda came out of the bedroom. Although she was still pouting, she took her place at the table. No one paid any particular attention to her until Becky spoke.

"I thought you weren't going to eat tonight."

Linda's gaze wavered and lowered to her plate.

Kay Orlis caught the younger girl's attention. "Becky."

But the towheaded youngster was not to be stopped so easily. "But that's what she told me, Auntie Kay. That's just exactly what she said. She wasn't going to eat supper tonight. She said so."

Linda's face was ashen, and her lips trembled uncertainly. "Becky! You be quiet."

"But you did so say that!"

Jim turned to Danny. "What's the matter?" he demanded. "What's going on, anyway?"

Nobody answered him.

He glanced at Linda. "Or is it supposed to be a secret or something?"

Danny warned him to be silent with his eyes. "That's enough," he ordered. "Now we won't be hearing any more of it."

Jim knew better than to voice his questions, but he still had them. Danny knew that.

Linda ate sparingly, and as soon as she was finished, she stood once more and hurried to her room. Once she was gone Jim turned curiously to Danny and Kay.

"Now," he said, "Will somebody please tell me what's goin' on around here? What's eatin' her, anyway?"

"The subject is closed," Danny told him.

* * *

The following day the baseball team had their first workout. Boyd Patterson and Jim Morgan both went out for the team, although Jim was so young that he practically knew he didn't have a chance of making it. That evening when he came home after practice, though, he was so excited about Boyd's pitching he could talk about little else.

"I tell you, Danny, you should just see him pitch. He's really got it."

"The paper said he looked good."

"Looked good? That's not the half of it. You never saw a high school pitcher with a curve ball like he's got. I don't think there's a batter on the team who can come within a mile of it when he's really in the groove."

Danny put aside the magazine he had been reading. "I had a hunch Boyd was going to do all right."

Jim Morgan pulled up a chair and sat down. "I thought Boyd was plenty sharp on the basketball court, but you should see him play baseball. I tell you, Danny, he's tops. If the rest of the team can give him a little help, we're going to be the next state champions."

Danny Orlis laughed good-naturedly. "That must've been quite a workout you had this afternoon, Jim. One practice session and already you're the state champions. What will you be doing by the time you've practiced a week?"

Jim Morgan's face reddened. "Just you wait, Danny," he exclaimed. "Just you wait until you see what Boyd can do with a baseball before you start talking like that. I can promise you this much right now. We're going to have the best baseball team you've ever seen."

Danny picked up his magazine and turned the pages absent-mindedly, but he did not start to read. "If Boyd gets to play baseball this year, Jim, you can thank Kay. The shape his grades were in, he wouldn't have been eligible if it hadn't been for Kay helping him with his studies."

"When the people around Fairview see what a terrific pitcher he is, everybody in town will be thanking her. He's going to *make* our team."

* * *

The following Thursday night they had the biggest turnout for the Bible club that they had had since it started. A few minutes before eight o'clock the kids started coming and kept piling in until they filled the living room. All the chairs in the house were in use and kids were sprawled on the floor in a ragged circle.

Danny Orlis led the Bible study. He gave them a brief summary of the events that led up to the portion they were studying and launched into **a** verse-by-verse discussion of it.

He tried to keep the lesson to an hour or **a** little less, but they asked so many questions that Danny was only a little more than half finished when the hour was over. He stopped and glanced at the clock.

"I didn't realize the time was going so fast," he confessed. "It looks as though our time for study is gone this evening. I think it would be best for us to quit now and take up where we're leaving off when we meet again next week."

Boyd Patterson spoke up quickly. "Some of us are in training, so we've got to be in early, Danny," he said, "but we've still got plenty of time. If you're game, I'd like to go on for another half an hour or so.

There are some more things I'd like to know about this passage we've been studying and I'm afraid that I'll forget what they are if we wait."

Linda Penner glanced in Boyd's direction and leaned forward admiringly. "I feel the same way," she agreed. "I think it would be wonderful if you'd go on, Danny – too wonderful for words."

Jim Morgan looked her way but did not voice his disgust. Somebody else snorted, and a girl near the door snickered aloud.

"We know you, Linda," she said. "You'd think anything that Boyd Patterson said was absolutely wonderful."

Hurt leaped to the older Penner girl's bewildered young eyes and her face flushed scarlet.

Danny Orlis broke in hurriedly. "If we're going to continue our study, we'd better get at it. If we don't, our time is apt to be gone and we won't be any farther along than we are now."

He looked Linda's way every now and then, but it was painfully obvious that she was not listening. Somehow, the brief exchange seemed to hurt the spirit of the study, and the last half-hour was dull and almost lifeless.

When they finished, the kids got up and, getting their coats, began to file out of the house. Danny and Kay Orlis stood near the door laughing and joking with the kids as they left. Neither of them missed Linda Penner until all the guests had gone. Kay looked around.

"There's going to be some cleaning to do here tomorrow," she said, "but that was a wonderful study, Danny. Especially the first hour. I believe some of those kids are beginning to get under conviction."

"Their questions were certainly pointed," he said. "And that's a good sign." Danny started toward a chair to sit down but paused. "Where's Linda?"

Jim Morgan's face was dark with disgust. "She went into her room as soon as you finished, Danny." He breathed deeply. "That Sue Bailey. She didn't have to spout off about Linda that way!"

"Am I hearing right, Jim?" Danny asked. "Am I really hearing you defending Linda?"

"I'm not exactly defending her," he said lamely. "It's just that Sue didn't have to make fun of Linda."

Kay looked at Danny. "Do you think I should go in and talk to her?"

He nodded. "Poor kid. That girl did give her a rough time."

Kay stood before the bedroom door momentarily, knocking lightly. "Linda," she called. "Linda."

There was no answer.

She knocked again.

Kay hesitated uncertainly, then opened the door and slipped inside. It was a moment or two before her eyes became accustomed to the darkness. Linda had thrown herself across the bed. She made no sound, but her shoulders twitched convulsively.

Kay Orlis moved quietly beside her. "Linda." Her own voice was little more than a whisper. "Linda."

Sitting on the edge of the bed she put her hand on the girl's shoulder. It was a moment or two before Linda acknowledged that Kay was there. Then she turned over and sat up, scrubbing her eyes.

"Oh, Kay," she exclaimed miserably. "I feel awful. They laughed at me! They laughed at me! I'll never be able to face any of them again."

Comfortingly Kay took her in her arms. Linda's scalding tears spilled down her cheeks and moistened the front of Kay's dress.

CHAPTER 5

SOMETHING NEW HAS BEEN ADDED

Neither Kay Orlis nor Linda Penner mentioned the incident that happened the night of the Bible club again, but it had a profound effect on their relationship. During the next few days, the bond between them seemed to grow almost daily. Previously, Kay had had to ask Linda every time she expected her to help with the housework, and then it was done only grudgingly.

But no more. Linda assumed the full responsibility for doing the dishes after meals without being told. And in addition, she began helping get Becky off to school, and keeping their room clean and the bed made. And, more and more, she began to seek Kay out when she had a problem and talk it over with her.

Danny Orlis noticed the change that had come over the girl so suddenly and asked Kay about it. "I'm curious, Kay. Has Linda made a decision for Christ? Is that why she's so different all of a sudden?"

Kay went to the door to make sure that both Penner girls were out of hearing distance before she answered Danny. "I only wish she had accepted Christ as her Savior," she said. "Then we would be making real, solid progress with her. But I am encouraged by the way she's accepting me. I think she's finally come to see that we do love her and want to help her." She shrugged her shoulders. "That's the only explanation I have."

Danny went to the kitchen cupboard and got a glass for a drink of water. "That Linda's an odd one. I always thought it was hard to understand boys, but believe me, boys are a cinch to figure out when you compare them with girls."

Kay made a little face at him.

He drew another glass of water from the faucet and sipped it thoughtfully. "Now that you're over that hurdle with Linda, maybe you'll be able to interest her in the things of the Lord. The way I see it, her problem is basically spiritual."

Kay's youthful face grew serious. "I know that, Danny," she agreed. "And winning her friendship isn't going to make any difference in the long run unless we can use it to point her to the Savior. But she has another problem that is very serious to her. She misses her mother more than even she herself realizes. She's growing up and needs someone older who has both experience and understanding to confide in."

Danny nodded. "I'm sure that God was leading when Linda and Becky came to live here," he agreed. "And, to tell you the absolute truth, Kay, I don't know of anyone better suited to give them advice and counsel than you are."

* * *

Bible club at Danny and Kay's went well again the following Thursday night. The kids packed the living room as they had the previous week, and two or three sat in the doorways.

As Danny taught the lesson the questions that were asked were deep and searching. One high school senior asked question after question about salvation and why it had been necessary for Christ to die on the Cross in order to save sinners.

Danny Orlis answered with Bible verses whenever he could. "The Bible tells us that no man who ever lived has been able to keep the law," he said. "Even Abraham. God said that He counted Abraham's faith as righteousness."

"'There is none righteous, not even one; there is none who understands, there is none who seeks for God;....'"

"In another place we're told that 'the wages of sin is death, but the free gift of God is eternal life in Christ Jesus our Lord.'"

Danny went on to explain how God had sent His Son to die on the Cross so that people everywhere might be saved.

"We cannot keep the law," he concluded, "because we are naturally sinful. God sent the Lord Jesus to live a perfect life and to be killed for our sins, so that we could put our trust in Him and be saved...."

When the lesson was finally over the kids got somberly to their feet and began to file out. Usually they laughed and joked a little, and Danny could count on several lingering to visit. But on this particular evening nobody had much to say. There was no joking at all. When they were all gone Kay turned to her young husband, eyes shining.

"Oh, Danny! Wasn't that wonderful?" she exclaimed. "Wasn't that the most thrilling lesson we've had for a long time?"

Danny took a long breath and expelled the air slowly. "It was just about as fine as any lesson we've ever had anywhere," he agreed, "even the Bible studies we used to have when we were in high school in Cedarton." He sat down and picked up his Bible. "If we could just have had some of those kids alone tonight," he said thoughtfully, "I'm almost sure someone would have come through for Christ. There were several who were certainly under conviction."

Kay straightened the chairs absentmindedly. "Even Linda was touched," she murmured.

Danny returned his Bible to the end table and got to his feet. "There's going to be a real break among the kids coming to the Bible club before very long. I'm convinced of it."

Before going to bed that night they knelt to pray as they always did. Only this time their prayers were different – more urgent.

* * *

The first of the following week Danny and Kay Orlis were somewhat surprised when Jim and Linda both came home from school excitedly, telling about a pleasant young man they had met at school that day. He had visited with several of the teachers and talked with quite a few of the kids after school, and came down to watch baseball practice for a time.

Jim Morgan had met him and talked with him for quite a while. He thought he was great. "I tell you, Danny, he's all right. He gave me a couple of pointers on my batting stance that helped a lot. He's a regular guy."

"He sure sounds like it," the youthful pilot said. "Where did you say he's from?"

Jim's forehead wrinkled. "He didn't say, I guess. But I think he must be from back east somewhere. At least he talked like it."

Danny Orlis continued his questioning without showing his concern. "Did anyone out at school know him?" he asked. "Anyone who had ever seen him before and knew his background and what he does?"

"Oh, sure," Jim retorted. "Mr. Lindstrom and Mr. Gruber both knew him, and a couple of the women teachers had seen him before. You don't need to worry about him, Danny. He's all right."

"What was he doing out at school?" he continued. "Did he have some special reason for being there or is he just visiting here?"

"Oh, no," Linda Penner broke in quickly, eyes sparkling and alive with excitement. "He's planning something big for Fairview. The biggest thing we've ever had around here."

"That's interesting." Danny measured his words carefully. "And just what is it he's going to do that's so big?"

Linda's voice grew louder. "He's going to put on a Christian Cavalcade."

Danny breathed deeply. "Christian Cavalcade?" he echoed. "What does he mean by that, Linda?"

There was a moment or two of hesitation. "I'm not exactly sure, but I know that it's going to be something big and–and beautiful. He was talking to some of us girls about it. He asked if we wanted to help him put it on."

Kay Orlis, who had been listening from the kitchen, came into the living room. "What is the purpose of it?" she asked. "What does he hope to accomplish?"

"He said he wanted to show the kids of the world that Christians could have just as good a program as the world can. He's going to show the kids out at school that there are some sharp people among the good Christians. So, he's going to bring in some really outstanding Christian personalities. People who sing and make records and – oh, it's going to be the biggest and best thing that's happened to Fairview!"

All Danny and Kay Orlis heard about at home the next few days was the Christian Cavalcade. Whatever it was, things were happening fast. Glenn Marsden had rented the Fairview Auditorium, appointed ushers, and was picking a choir to help with the singing. Linda, who had never seemed interested in spiritual things before and acted as though she only went to church because she had to, was particularly impressed. When she came home from school she was bubbling with excitement.

"Oh, Kay, it's going to be the most wonderful program that's ever been held in Fairview," she said. "Everybody out at school is excited about it. All the girls think that Mr. Marsden's real cute."

Jim Morgan came in and sat down. "It sounds like it's going to be a big deal, all right. The whole school is talking about it – if that means anything."

Linda Penner hitched closer to Kay, her dark eyes sparkling. "Mr. Marsden showed *me* the pictures of some of the women who are coming here for the program. Are they ever beautiful!" She turned to Jim. "Aren't they, Jim?"

He grunted. "How would you expect me to know that?"

"You do, too, know. I saw you looking at the pictures the same as I did."

His young face flushed, and his voice was defensive. "That was only because Glenn Marsden asked me to look at 'em. But I didn't see anything so beautiful about them. They just looked like girls to me."

Linda Penner bristled. "I suppose if they'd been in baseball uniforms and carried a catcher's mitt or a bat you'd have been more interested."

Jim's eyebrows raised in horror. "Oh, no!" he spoke quickly. "I should say not. It's bad enough having to put up with women everywhere else. I sure wouldn't want to see them playing baseball, too."

Danny chuckled.

"What do you think about this Christian Cavalcade, Danny?" Jim asked after a moment or two. "I haven't heard you say a single thing about it."

"That's probably because I don't know anything about it," he replied.

"You know as much about it as anyone else in town knows," Jim told him.

Danny did not answer immediately.

Kay's gaze sought his. "What do you think of it?" she asked.

He cleared his throat. "I don't honestly know what to say. I hate to say anything about any Christian effort unless I know a lot more about it than I know about this Christian Cavalcade." He uncrossed his legs and sat up. "The question we've got to ask ourselves is this. Is it going to glorify God and bring honor to Him, or is it going to bring honor to man?"

"What do you mean by that?" Linda asked defensively.

"Frankly," Danny continued, "I have some reservations about anything that is carried out in the way I am afraid this affair is going to be carried out. But I certainly wouldn't want to pass a definite opinion until I know a lot more about it than I do."

Linda ruffled. "I think Christians should have things just as nice as the world does," she declared. "There isn't any reason for us to leave all the good times and good entertainment to the world."

"I'm sure the Christian has more good times than a person in the world ever does," Danny answered, getting to his feet. "And as far as the Christian Cavalcade is concerned, we'll just have to wait and see."

Linda's voice was sharp. "You sound just like Daddy. He's just naturally against everything I like."

Danny changed the subject.

CHAPTER 6

CONFLICT!

The next Thursday night Danny and Kay Orlis had their Bible club again, but the crowd was down considerably. Danny came into the living room at eight o'clock and looked around, disappointment marring his face.

"Where is everybody?" he asked.

Jim Morgan answered him. "I thought I told you, Danny," he explained. "Mr. Marsden was having a meeting of the committees for the Christian Cavalcade and that took a lot of our kids."

Danny pulled up a chair and sat down.

"It was the only night they could have it, Danny." Jim spoke defensively. "Last night was prayer meeting and there's something going on at school tomorrow night."

"What about Saturday night?" Kay put in.

"That's always a bad night to get anybody out to anything. Mr. Marsden just had to have the meeting tonight."

Danny Orlis acted as though he was about to reply, but stopped and got his Bible. "I'm very thankful that you kids came to club tonight," he said. "And I hope I didn't give you the impression I'm scolding you for the ones who didn't come – or that I'm scolding them, either. I guess I'm just a little disappointed….

He tried hard, but somehow the lesson bogged down. The kids were listless and asked few questions, and there was scarcely any discussion. Previously the lessons had seemed short when they ran more than an hour, but this evening the lesson dragged on endlessly. Danny finally drew it to a close fifteen minutes short of an hour.

When the kids went home, he and Kay made their way to their bedroom. He dropped to a chair wearily and untied his shoes. Concern darkened his eyes.

"What was the matter tonight?" he asked. "Why wouldn't the study go?"

She came over and stood beside him. "The size of the crowd was down for one thing," she suggested. "That always makes a difference."

Danny shook his head. "Not in Bible club," he countered. "I think some of the best meetings we've had have been meetings that were poorly attended." He shook his head. "Nope, it was something else." There was a moment's silence. "And last week some of those same kids who were here tonight seemed to be so close to making a decision for Christ. Tonight, they were like a bunch of cold fish."

She spoke softly in reply. "What do *you* think it is?"

Danny reached up and covered her tiny hand with his. "I hate to say it, Kay, but I wonder if it could be this Christian Cavalcade. It's taking the attention and interest of a lot of kids. It could just be the thing that is getting them to take their eyes off the Lord."

"But this project has a good purpose, Danny. It's aimed at challenging kids for Christ."

"Is it?" He looked up at her searchingly. "I've been piecing this thing together, Kay. I don't know this Glenn Marsden. He sounds like a very sincere Christian and I'm sure that everything he is doing is with the very best of motives. I'm sure he is sincerely interested in reaching kids for Christ."

"He's certainly getting Linda's attention, if that means anything."

"But," Danny Orlis continued, "I still have a big question mark in my mind about the whole project. It seems to me that he's trying to win kids to Christ by putting on a bigger and better show than the world does."

Kay stiffened. "Danny, is that fair?" she asked. "Should you judge Mr. Marsden and his project that way?"

"I hope I'm wrong." He got to his feet and crossed to the other door. "But that's the way it looks to me. Every time the kids come home, they bring some new big name in Christian music. The person is supposed to be coming for the Christian Cavalcade, or Marsden is trying to get him, or wishes he could get him. That sounds to me as though he's putting his trust in the talent of men rather than in God."

"Those people are using their talents to serve the Lord," she reminded him, "in the same way as you are using your ability to fly."

"I know you're right about that, Kay." Danny ran his fingers through his crew cut. "And I'm probably not explaining myself very well. I'm not talking about the people he's bringing in. That's not it at all. I'm sure the motives of most of them are of the very best. The thing that disturbs me is the way he's going about this thing."

"What do you mean?"

"He seems to feel that all he has to do is to get enough outstanding talent and put on the finest show possible and people will be saved."

"I'd never thought of it in quite that way."

"Then there's this stress on production. He's got a crew of 'stagehands' and is training a couple of boys to operate the spotlights for the program. He's using fancy backgrounds and expensive costuming. I haven't been around worldly stage productions, but I know enough about them to know that's exactly the way they operate." He took a long breath. "I hope I'm wrong, Kay," he sighed, "but I'm desperately concerned."

The following afternoon the Fairview baseball team played its opening game. It was a raw April day and only a handful of townspeople braved the harsh wind to come out and watch them play. Danny Orlis had been scheduled to fly to Saskatchewan that morning, but bad weather had grounded him, so he and Kay were able to go out and watch Jim Morgan and Boyd.

Jim was a utility outfielder and so didn't get in the starting lineup, but Boyd was the starting pitcher and did a masterful job of handcuffing the opposition. The first eight batters he set down in order before giving up a little pop single to right field.

A bit of chatter went up from the handful of fans who had come over from Bison Lake to watch the game.

Boyd took the throw from the fielder, looked calmly over at first to check the runner, and directed his attention to the plate. The base runner took a lead off first. In a quick, rifle-like throw he snapped the ball to the first baseman. The runner started back, but not in time. Boyd nailed him a foot off the bag for the final out of the inning.

Danny Orlis glanced in Kay's direction, grinning admiringly. "Jim was sure right about Boyd Patterson. That kid is plenty good."

The next inning Fairview got a man on first with a walk. The next batter rapped a sharp single that almost got away from the left fielder and sent the runners scampering to second and third. Boyd Patterson came up to bat.

Danny glanced in Kay's direction, exclaiming, "Just watch him! He acts like an old pro who's been in a situation like this hundreds of times."

Boyd scuffed the dirt in the batter's box with his

toe and balanced the bat with calm eagerness. The first ball came whistling in. Boyd sized it up shrewdly and let it go by.

"Ball one," the umpire cried.

The next pitch headed for the inside corner. Boyd swung strongly. The bat met the ball with a resounding crack and slammed it over the center fielder's head. It bounced off the fence and the fielder scrambled for it as Boyd raced for third. He touched the keystone sack and sped for home. The throw came in, but it was too late and low. The pitcher cut it off.

Danny Orlis shouted above the din around them, "What did I tell you, Kay? Boyd Patterson is going to burn up the league!"

* * *

The next issue of the Fairview Times carried a long article about the baseball victory over Bison Lake and a shorter feature about Boyd Patterson and the other teams he had played for in the past. Jim Morgan, who had seen action late in the game, turned to the sports page as soon as he got home and showed it to Danny Orlis.

"Danny, did you read what they wrote about Boyd?"

"How could I?" the young pilot asked good-naturedly. "You've had the paper ever since it came."

"Aw...."

"What do they say?" Danny asked. "That he played a good game?"

"I'll say they do." Jim read a paragraph over silently. "It's a funny thing, but the sports editor sounds as though he's surprised that Boyd did so well. It didn't surprise me, though. I knew he was going to burn the old apple in to those guys."

"You've got to admit, he did all right," Danny acknowledged.

Jim Morgan laughed loudly. "You can say that again. Three hits. That's all they got off him. Three lousy little hits. And Bison Lake was supposed to outclass us so far with the hickory. I guess we woke up a few guys."

Danny looked down at the picture of Boyd that the newspaper had used.

"Boyd's sure getting the publicity. I hope he can take it without getting bigheaded."

"You aren't going to have to worry about Boyd ever gettin' bigheaded. He doesn't pay any attention to the stuff they write about him."

Danny straightened in his chair. "That's fine," he cautioned, "but let me tell you something, Jim. I've seen a lot of young guys who started out modest and unconceited, but who couldn't take it. I've seen them begin to believe all the things they read about themselves. And when that happens it can do a guy a lot of harm."

"I know." Jim Morgan was still unconvinced. "But I still say that we don't have to worry about Boyd Patterson. He's not going to get swellheaded over anything. He's too much of a regular guy."

CHAPTER 7

THE BIG NIGHT

After the next meeting of the Christian Cavalcade committee, the kids fanned out over Fairview distributing tickets and accepting contributions. Linda Penner hurried home to beat Jim Morgan to Danny and Kay.

"You'll get your tickets to the Cavalcade from me, won't you, Kay?" she pleaded.

Kay Orlis frowned. "Do you mean you're *selling* tickets for it?" The thought seemed unbelievable. "Since it's a Christian program, I just assumed that it would be free."

"It is free. That is, the tickets are free," she explained. "But Mr. Marsden said we were getting top quality singers so we should try to get some of the adults to make contributions when they get their tickets."

Kay said no more about it to Linda but talked it over with Danny at the first opportunity.

"Well, Kay," he said, "at least it isn't a moneymaking scheme. I'm sure of that. When you check through the list of people that this chap, Marsden, is bringing in, you can see that he's going to have a hard time even getting enough money to pay the expenses. A program like this isn't going to be cheap to produce."

"I suppose you're right," Kay hesitatingly replied, "but somehow, I don't like the idea of giving someone a ticket then immediately asking him to make a contribution, especially in a Christian operation. And I don't think others are going to go for it, either."

"Maybe not."

Nevertheless, interest in the Christian Cavalcade continued to grow. Both Jim Morgan and Linda Penner distributed all of their tickets the very first day and went back for more. Surprisingly, a lot of people made generous contributions. Jim, who hadn't been more than casually interested after Danny expressed himself, became more and more excited about it as the time for the program grew closer.

"I think everybody in town is going to be there." he said enthusiastically, "This is going to be a really big deal. We've never had anything like it in Fairview, or anywhere else we've ever lived. It's the greatest."

"It sure sounds that way."

"I haven't been so keen on it until the last couple of days, Danny," he went on, "but I've sure changed my mind. I tell you, it's going to be wonderful. I think a lot of kids are going to get an entirely different idea of what Christianity really is just by seeing this program."

Danny Orlis started to reply but checked himself.

That evening when the kids were in bed and Danny and Kay were finally alone, they talked about the Cavalcade again.

"The kids are really getting excited about it, aren't they?" Kay questioned.

Danny nodded. "I can't help thinking about tomorrow night's Bible club," he said. "I wonder what sort of a crowd we'll have."

"I don't know," she answered. "Mr. Marsden is keeping the kids awfully busy."

Danny took off his suit coat and put it on a hanger. "That's what I'm afraid of. He keeps them so busy they don't have time to attend a Bible club where the Word of God is taught."

The next morning at breakfast Jim Morgan brought up the matter of postponing Bible club. "We've got so much work to do on this Christian Cavalcade that it's going to be rough to find time even to get to club tonight, Danny. Don't you think it would be a good idea to postpone it for once?"

Danny shook his head. "No, Jim, I can't go along with that. I don't think it's wise to postpone club. If we do that it's apt to be just that much harder to get the kids into the habit of coming again."

Jim shrugged his shoulders. "All right," he said offhandedly, "but don't be too surprised if nobody shows up. We've got an awful lot to do to get that program ready to put on."

Although they held Bible club at the usual time that evening only a handful showed up. Boyd Patterson was there with a friend of his. A couple of girls who had just moved to town came to see what it was like, and Jim and Linda Penner were there. That was all. The new girls looked around distastefully.

"There certainly aren't very many here," one of them said, turning to Linda. "I thought you said there would be lots of kids." "There usually are lots of kids here for club," Linda explained lamely, "but everybody's working on the Cavalcade. We wanted to postpone club just this once, but *he* wouldn't do it." With a nod of her head, she indicated Danny.

Danny started the lesson and tried valiantly, but the kids weren't with him. Actually, it was worse than it had been the week before if that was possible. Every time there was a lull Linda or someone else turned to a neighbor with a question or remark about the Christian Cavalcade. Doggedly Danny stumbled through the lesson and closed with prayer.

There was a short silence. Then Linda turned to the new girl sitting closest to her.

"You might find the Bible club a little dull," she apologized, "but you won't find the Christian Cavalcade that way. It's going to be wonderful. You've never been to anything quite like it."

Jim broke in quickly. "By the way, do you have

your tickets yet? It's going to be great. Everybody in town will be there."

"Jim!" Linda exploded. "They're *my* customers. **I** talked to them first."

The girls laughed.

"Somebody already beat you to it," one of them said. "We've already got our tickets. But how come you're all fighting to use up the most tickets? What good's that going to do?"

"Oh, there's a reason for it," Linda answered. "The ones who distribute the most tickets and bring in the biggest contributions get to ride downtown in the same convertibles with the singers. Isn't that neat?"

"Say," Boyd's friend said, "maybe I should get in on that, too. Is it too late to start now?"

Danny was sick with disappointment when the kids left. "It looks as though we should've postponed Bible club tonight after all," he said wearily.

Jim nodded. "That's what I told you, Danny. It isn't that the kids aren't interested in club. They're just so busy now they simply don't have the time." He read the disappointment in Danny's eyes. "But don't worry about it. Just you wait until after the Cavalcade. There'll be so many kids coming to club that we won't be able to get them all in the house. We may have to move club down to the church or to the Municipal Building."

Danny spoke doubtfully and without enthusiasm. "I hope you're right."

The Christian Cavalcade came off on Monday night

of the following week. By any human standards that anyone could apply to it, it was a tremendous success. The auditorium was filled to capacity fifteen minutes before time for the program to begin. Danny and Kay Orlis, arriving about 7:30, took seats near the front.

"You know, Kay, I am surprised," Danny admitted. "There are people here who I would have thought would never come to anything Christian. But they're here tonight."

She nodded but did not reply.

Presently the lights dimmed, and the curtain started up. An instant later the spotlight came on to highlight an attractive young soprano in a dazzling white gown. A murmur of acclaim ran through the crowd and the kids started to clap.

From that beginning, the program moved along rapidly from entertainer to entertainer. The audience waxed enthusiastic. They clapped loudly for encore after encore, and here and there a few whistled or moaned in the accepted rock 'n roll crowd manner.

Kay turned to Danny. "Do you like this?" she asked.

He shook his head. "I can't say that I do," he answered softly. "It's not my idea of a program that honors the Lord."

"Nor mine," she agreed. There was a moment's hesitation. "But we must remember that so many of these young people who are here tonight have not had any religious training."

"I suppose you're right at that."

At the intermission Mr. Marsden announced that each one of the entertainers had a good supply of CDs with them and that they would be on sale at the close of the program. Then, to the disgust of Danny and some of the others, the next fifteen minutes was used in a plea for a sizable offering so all the bills could be paid.

The last half of the program was almost the same as the first. It was superbly staged, moved rapidly from one number to the next, with a fine change of pace, and came to a climax with a message. Glenn Marsden came on stage himself and gave a short, tastefully done sermonette. He outlined the plan of salvation and gave his own personal testimony.

A final number and the curtain went down, and the houselights came on. For a moment or two Danny and Kay Orlis remained seated.

"What do you think now, Danny?" she asked.

He was slow in answering. "I still say that there's no denying Marsden's sincerity," he said. "And I'm sure that his whole purpose is to try to challenge these kids for Christ."

"But you aren't sure whether you approve of what's gone on here tonight; is that it?"

They were speaking quietly so that no one else could hear them.

"I know what I think of what we've seen tonight," Danny answered, "but I'm not sure whether it is right or not. I really don't like to judge the efforts of others to reach the lost with the Gospel of Christ."

Kay stood up and Danny helped her with her coat.

"I think I know exactly how you feel. I feel the same way, but I can't tell you just why."

As they reached the aisle a guy and his date pushed ahead of them.

"What did you think of it, Judy?" the boy was asking his girl.

She grinned up at him. "I liked it fine," she said, "all excepting the commercial. I didn't dig that preaching they had to stick on the end. As far as I'm concerned, they sure wrecked a terrific show by bringing that religious sermon at the end."

"That's the way I felt, too. I didn't like the idea of all that preachin', but the show was the greatest. A lot better than they have at the Bijou Theater – and a lot cheaper, too."

Danny and Kay Orlis left the school auditorium in silence and made their way to their old car. Becky was with them, but they had to wait briefly for Jim Morgan and Linda Penner. Danny put the key in the ignition and turned to his young wife.

"Well, was it what you thought it was going to be, Kay?"

She shook her head. "I don't know exactly what I expected, but somehow it was so–so gaudy." She paused. "And they seemed to spend a lot of time talking about the ability of the various entertainers and their accomplishments."

"That was one of the first things that bothered me, too," Danny admitted. "I'm sure most of the people who appeared on the program are very sincere, and in spite of the stress that was put on getting a good offering, they probably didn't take in more than enough to pay the expenses. The thing that disturbed me the worst, though, was the fact that the whole emphasis seemed to be wrong. It was on men and women and what they had done, instead of on Christ and what He has done for us." Danny paused momentarily and took a deep breath. "Then there was the way they used stage production and spotlights. The program was put together like a big production – a show. A lot of work went into it, but I got the distinct impression that the cause of Christ wasn't benefited a great deal by what took place tonight."

At that moment Jim Morgan and Linda Penner came running to the car. Linda was still so excited she could scarcely talk.

"Wasn't that program super?" she blurted.

Jim Morgan glanced at her approvingly. "You can say that again, Linda. It was great. I sure would like to have some of the CDs they sold. They were really great."

"It was the most wonderful, the most exciting program I've ever been to. I got all their autographs, Kay. Every one of them."

"Can I see them, Linda?" Becky asked. "Can I?"

"As soon as we get home." She leaned back in the seat and closed her eyes. "Oh, that program was absolutely marvelous."

Danny started the engine and backed out of the parking lot.

"You know," Linda added, "if church was like that all the time I wouldn't *mind* going."

Danny started to reply but changed his mind. Jim and Linda talked endlessly about the program. As Danny drove into the yard and stopped, Linda addressed him.

"I'll bet anything this will help the attendance at Bible club, Danny," she said. "Now that these kids have found out that Christians aren't 'square' there'll be a lot of kids who'll want to come to club."

"I hope so," Danny said thoughtfully.

It was not until they were in the house that he spoke again. "I'll say this. There were sure a lot of kids, and older people, too, at the meeting tonight who had never heard the Gospel before. We should be praying for them."

Linda Penner started for the room she shared with Becky. At the door she stopped and turned. "Danny," she asked, "when do you think we'll have another Christian Cavalcade?"

CHAPTER 8

WHERE IS EVERYBODY?

The following Thursday night Kay Orlis got ready for Bible club again. She was just baking a batch of brownies when Danny came home from the airport. He picked up a brownie and sampled it.

"Not bad. It's a good thing you have the kids coming over once in a while, so I get something good to eat."

Kay wrinkled her nose at him. "I feel sorry for you."

He took another brownie and perched on a stool in the kitchen. "Well," he questioned, "how many kids do you think we'll have at the meeting tonight?"

"Jim and Linda both said they thought I should bake plenty of brownies. They talked as though half the kids in high school would be coming."

Boyd Patterson was the first to come over after dinner, his English book under his arm.

"I almost didn't come tonight," he said. "I spent so much time helping with the Cavalcade that I'm about bushed. But I've got to have some help with my English again."

Kay dried her hands on the corner of a towel.

A few minutes before eight the kids began to straggle in by ones and twos. Jim noted the time and turned to Danny.

"I can't understand it, Danny," he moaned. "Everybody I talked to *said* they were coming."

Boyd nodded. "That's what they said this morning, but I talked with a couple of guys tonight and they said they'd been working so hard on the Cavalcade they wouldn't be able to come. They just had to stay at home and study."

"But club only lasts an hour," Jim said, disappointment edging his voice.

"When you're flunking English and want to play baseball an hour's an hour – even if it does make a guy miss club."

Danny picked up his Bible. "It's a little after eight," he said. "I think we'd better get started."

One of the guys leaned over to Jim and whispered hoarsely, "This is pretty dull stuff after that Cavalcade. I think I'd like club better if we could have a little excitement."

Danny continued as though he had not heard the remark.

Jim and Boyd and a couple of others entered the discussion, but again the lesson dragged endlessly. When it was over Danny was heartsick.

"I prepared as well as ever, Kay," he sighed, "and we've been praying for club – perhaps even harder than we did a few weeks ago. But we haven't had any response at all. I don't know what's the matter."

Kay Orlis tried to conceal her own discouragement. "Everybody is so tired tonight, Danny. Maybe things will be better next week."

He straightened slowly. "I'd hate to blame this on the Christian Cavalcade," he said, "but there's a feeling here I can't quite understand. The kids act as though they're dissatisfied with club now – that it isn't exciting enough."

Kay came over and put her arm around him. "We'll just have to pray a little harder for them, Danny."

"I know that's the answer, but the thing that disturbs me most is that some of the kids were so close to making a decision for Christ before all of this began to happen. Sometimes I wonder if they'll ever come that close again."

* * *

The weather was good for flying the next few days and Danny Orlis was in the air almost constantly. He made two trips to Minneapolis with Dr. Gordon, a rush flight to Ontario with supplies, and a trip to northern Saskatchewan to make emergency repairs on the Cessna 180 the mission used to supply their stations in the bush. If Danny was home at all, he came in late and was gone again early the next morning.

During that period baseball and the coming game with Forest City were the topic of conversation all over Fairview. Every night Jim Morgan came home with the latest addition to the running account.

"Know what the guys uptown are saying, Kay?" he asked. "They think we'll have the championship in the bag if we can only knock off Forest City Saturday afternoon. Boy, that's going to be some game! I can hardly wait!"

"If you keep talking like that," Kay told him jokingly, "you'll have me excited about it, too."

"Everybody in town is excited. Do you know what it means to win the district title, Kay? Fairview has never done it before. Not even once."

Every evening after dinner Boyd Patterson came over to get Kay's help on his studies. Jim watched with growing concern, until he could contain himself no longer. He went into the kitchen with exaggerated carelessness and sat down across from the star pitcher.

"How're things going, Boyd?" he asked.

"All right, I guess."

"You sure looked sharp tonight against us reserves. You'll slaughter Forest City."

Boyd's frown deepened. "The way things are going now I might not even get to play."

Shock darkened Jim's eyes. "You don't mean that," he said helplessly. "You–you're just kiddin'."

Boyd pushed the book aside and looked up. "I wish I was just kiddin'. But I've got to pass a stiff test or I'm not going to get to play at all. I won't even get to suit up."

"I–I thought everything was going all right for you in the grade department."

"It was for a while," Boyd said, "but then I went out for baseball and got started helping with the Christian Cavalcade. I guess I quit studying as much as I should've. Anyway, I'm sure in deep trouble now."

"You've got to pass that test, Boyd! If you don't, we're sunk!"

Kay Orlis spent as much time as possible helping Boyd. So much time, in fact, that she didn't pay the attention to Linda she should have. The dark-haired girl came into the kitchen shortly after finishing the dishes, her sweater over her arm.

"I'm going down to the library, Kay," she said.

Kay looked up.

"I've got some reading to do in Social Studies," she explained.

"I thought you went to the library to do that last night."

The girl's cheeks colored daintily and when she spoke, she was hesitant. "I–I did, but when I got there somebody else was using the book and–and I didn't get to do anything with it."

Kay noted the time. "All right, Linda," she agreed, "but I think you'd better be in by 9:30 tonight."

"I'll try." Her voice was flippant.

"I'm going to expect you back at 9:30, Linda. If you can't make it by then you had better stay home."

For a brief instant defiance leaped to Linda's snapping dark eyes, and her lips curled scornfully. "I'll be back at 9:30, but I don't know what I've done to keep you from trusting me. Actually, Kay, you treat me as though I'm no older than Becky."

With that she hurried out the kitchen door.

Although Linda Penner had promised Kay that she would be back home by 9:30, it was almost 10:45 when she finally came in. Danny and Kay were waiting up for her. Just inside the door she stopped and looked from one to the other.

"What's the matter?" she demanded innocently. "What's wrong?"

"Do you realize what time it is?" Danny asked.

Her pretty face went blank. "I–I didn't look at my watch," she said, "but it–it can't be so very late. A couple of the girls and I went out for a dish of ice cream after the library closed. We'd been studying *so* hard."

His expression did not change. "Where did you go, Linda?"

"Don't you believe me?"

"Where did you go?" Danny insisted.

She swallowed hard. "To–to the drugstore."

Danny's voice was kind, but very stern. "The drugstore closes at nine o'clock."

Linda's cheeks flushed scarlet. "Oh–I–I–"

"The truth is that you didn't go to the library at all, did you?"

Tears came to Linda's eyes. "I did go to the library." Her voice quavered. "And if you don't believe it, you can ask some of the girls. That's the trouble. You always think I'm telling you something that isn't true. You don't trust me."

Kay moistened her lips as though to speak, but Danny continued before she had an opportunity to say anything.

"We would like to trust you, Linda," he told her. "But trust is something that has to be earned." He went over to a chair and sat down. "Sit down for a minute. I'd like to talk to you."

She did as she was told.

"If you went to the library tonight," he continued, "it was to meet a boy."

"I–"

He handed her the paper. "Before you tell me something else that isn't true, read this. According to this reporter the library will be reopened tomorrow after being closed for redecorating."

Linda Penner flushed scarlet. Her lips trembled uncertainly. But there was defiance in her voice – defiance and indignation. "If you'd let me do things like the other kids get to do, I wouldn't have to lie to you. But you won't. You've got to treat me like a baby! I can't do anything and have any fun." She got to her feet. "Anybody would get into trouble living around you two. You don't want me to go to shows. You don't want me to dance. You don't want me to do anything. You'd even crab at me if I didn't do anything except go to prayer meeting."

Quite deliberately, Danny Orlis stood. His eyes blazed with authority and when he spoke his voice was crisp and firm. "That's enough, Linda. I can't let you talk to Kay and me the way you're doing, and you're so angry that it won't do any good for you to talk with us now. We'll finish this conversation in the morning after you've had an opportunity to think things through."

Her gaze lowered briefly, but she did not move. "What's wrong with finishing right now?" she demanded. "All you've got to do is tell me how many months I'll be grounded. Or am I so bad you're going to send me to the girls' reformatory?"

"Linda." His voice rose slightly. "I'm not going to tell you again. Go to your room."

She hesitated briefly, as though weighing the force in his voice. Then her eyes flooded with tears, and she turned away. "I'm tired of being treated like a baby. Nobody trusts me or cares what happens to me. I'd just as well be dead."

Danny did not reply.

When Linda was gone Kay turned to him. "I suppose you had to talk so sternly to her." Reluctance edged her voice.

"We owe it to Henry to teach her to respect authority, Kay," he declared. "If we don't, she's going to be headed for real trouble. She's got to be brought into hand."

"I know that. Only it makes me feel badly that we have to do it. The poor girl is really miserable."

"Most people in sin are miserable, Kay," he reminded her. "Only they usually try to hide it." He lowered his voice. "I can't believe that Linda has drifted very far into sin, but we've got to get hold of her now – before she does get into something really bad. And she's just the sort of girl who could do it."

Kay Orlis nodded her agreement. "How do you plan to punish her, Danny?"

"I'm not exactly sure." He spoke slowly. "What do you think about keeping her home at nights for a couple of weeks, except for activities at church?"

"That seems harsh," Kay said, "but she did lie to us in a deliberate attempt to deceive us."

NEW THRILLS

The next morning Jim Morgan was walking down the street to school when Boyd Patterson yelled to him.

"Hey, Jim! Wait a sec!"

The Morgan boy stopped and waited until his friend joined him. "What's up?" Jim asked.

"I got a letter from Forest City. They're going to have a Christian Cavalcade just like we had."

Jim's eyes brightened. "Honest? Boy, that's great."

"And what's more, they want us to come over and help them put it on."

Jim scratched his head. "I don't know whether Danny and Kay will let me do that," he said. "It took an awful lot of time to put ours on and we'd have to go out of town and everything – probably even on school nights when we should be studying."

Boyd Patterson fished the letter from his pocket and handed it to Jim. "It's just like this letter says," he continued, "we've got to consider it as missionary work. It's a chance for us to reach some of the kids over in Forest City for Christ."

They crossed the street and went into the sprawling brick building.

"I suppose that's right. What do your parents think about it, Boyd?"

For a brief instant Boyd's eyes clouded. "They don't understand at all," he said. "To tell you the truth, they never have understood much about Christian things. Dad just says he's afraid I'll get so busy I won't be able to keep up my studies. That's all it means to him."

"That reminds me," Jim answered. "How're you doin' in English?"

Boyd grimaced. "As well as I'll ever be able to do. English is one subject I just can't get hold of. I don't do any better on it than I do Algebra."

"You'd better get hold of it well enough to keep your grades up," Jim countered. "You know what'll happen to our baseball team if you don't. We've got to have you out there on the pitcher's mound or everybody'll clobber us."

"You sound just like my dad," Boyd said, laughing. "But don't worry, Jim. I'll see that I don't get into that mess again. I've had my fill of that."

At school several other kids had gotten letters from the Christian Cavalcade in Forest City. As soon as Jim and Boyd entered the building a couple of girls came hurrying over to them.

"Did you hear the news?" The voice of the girl speaking shrilled with excitement. "We've got invitations to help Forest City put on a big program like we did."

Boyd took his letter from his pocket. "Yeh, I know. I got a letter, too. Sounds like a big deal, doesn't it?"

"Oh, I'm so excited I can hardly wait to get over there and get to work. I don't think I ever had so much fun helping with something. It was a lot better than the musical we put on here at school last year."

* * *

Linda Penner took Danny Orlis' pronouncement of her punishment without comment. She shrugged her shoulders indifferently when he told her she was not to go anywhere except to church activities for a period of two weeks.

If they thought she was going to show how much it hurt to be grounded, they were going to be surprised. She wasn't going to give them that satisfaction. The punishment itself was bad enough, but the way Danny treated her was even worse. He acted as though she was a baby – younger than Becky, even.

Come to think of it, he even treated Becky better than he did her.

She'd talk to Dad, that's what she'd do. As soon as he got home from his route she'd go over and see him. He had never treated her that way himself. If he knew the way Danny was picking on her, he'd let her move back and keep house for him.

A faint smile twisted her pouting young lips.

Then she'd show Danny, and Kay, too. And she wouldn't have to lie to get out of the house once in a while. She could do just as she pleased and nobody would say a word.

All day Linda thought of little else. She had to stay at home for two weeks. Two whole weeks. Imagine! She fumed inwardly. "I'll die. If Daddy doesn't let me move back home with him, I'll just die!" she said inwardly.

She had a test that afternoon, but she was so hurt and angry that she only half tried. "I'll show them. I'll show them all!"

That afternoon as she left the school a couple of older boys were standing out by their car, smoking. She smiled at them. "Hi."

Jack Ross, the older of the two, took a deep drag on his cigarette and looked her over critically. "Not bad," he said. "Not bad at all."

Linda Penner colored and would have gone by, but he stepped out in front of her.

"Say, Cutie, where've you been all my life? How come I've never noticed you around before?"

"I've been here all the time."

Stay Grayson laughed. "You've never been down in the kindergarten before, Jack. That's the reason you've never seen her."

Linda flushed scarlet.

Jack Ross glowered at him. "Quiet. If I want your remarks, I'll ask for them." He turned to Linda. "How about it, Doll, would you like a ride home?"

Linda dimpled at him. "It sounds like fun."

Jack Ross went around to his side of the car and got in. She stood there momentarily. After a brief instant he reached over and opened the door on her side.

"Hurry it up. I haven't got all day."

She got in quickly.

Jack backed away from the curb, threw the car into low gear and roared away. She caught her breath.

He grinned at her. "Like that, huh?"

She forced a smile to her thin lips. "It–it's fun," she managed lamely.

He braked sharply as he approached the intersection, cornered on screeching tires, and lurched to a stop behind a slow-moving car. One hand on the horn, he whipped past the other vehicle and continued on his way.

"Know something? You sound like my kind of girl. Where've you been all my life?"

Her smile came back slowly. "I already told you. Around."

"Just wait until we get out of town and I'll really give you a thrill. I've been tuning this old crate up. She'll beat anything in town. Why, there isn't another guy out at school who'll race me."

"I–I'd like to go for a ride, Jack, but I can't make it now. I've got to get home."

He looked at her suspiciously. "You aren't feeding me a line, are you?"

"No, I'm not!" Her voice raised in protest. "I'm telling you the truth. Honestly, I am."

"You sound scared to me." Scorn edged his voice.

"Me, scared?" she countered. "You don't know me very well if you think that. It–it would take more than a fast car ride to scare me." Suddenly, pleasing Jack Ross came to mean more to her than anything else in the world. "I'm really excited about going for a fast ride with you, but I'm living with an old ogre who'll eat me alive if I'm not home right after school."

"You mean you don't live with your parents?"

She shook her head, and for an instant or two self-pity welled within her. "Mother's dead and Dad has to be gone all the time," she explained, "so he's got Becky and me staying with those horrible Orlis people."

Jack Ross sneered. "Orlis? Seems as though I've heard of him. He's the guy who flies for that missionary outfit, isn't he?"

She nodded.

"That guy!" Jack Ross snorted. "I'd like to teach him a thing or two."

Linda looked up at him helplessly. "And Jack, I–I think you'd better let me off around the corner so they won't see me getting out of the car."

He frowned darkly but did as she had asked. "If I can't call the house, how can I get in touch with you again?"

"I can talk to one of my girlfriends and see if you can phone her to relay any messages. Or, maybe we can meet at school."

"Good enough."

She opened the car door and started to get out. "If you do see me at school, Jack, don't let Jim Morgan see you talking to me. He's as fanatical as they are. He tattles everything I do."

She told Jack goodbye and started to the house. For a brief moment remorse swept over her. She hadn't told Jack the truth about Danny and Kay. They were fanatical enough about religion, and all of that, but they weren't really mean to her. She slowed her pace. Still, if making her stay home nights for two whole weeks wasn't being mean, she didn't know what was.

Kay was in the kitchen when she entered.

"Hello, Linda."

The girl took her books into the bedroom and laid them on the dresser. "I'd have been home from school a lot sooner," she lied, "but some of the girls and I went uptown and had a dish of ice cream. Time went so fast it was late before I realized it."

"That's all right. Danny and Jim aren't here yet, either."

CHAPTER 10

DECISIONS, DECISIONS, DECISIONS!

The night before Bible club Jim Morgan went into the living room and sat down across from Danny Orlis. "Did I tell you that Forest City is having a Christian Cavalcade and wants some of us to help with it?" he asked.

Danny looked up from the paper. "I heard you and Linda talking about it, but I didn't know what it was all about."

Jim hesitated. "It's not that I'm so crazy about helping, but they don't have more than a handful of Christian kids over there. I don't think they'd be able to put on the program if it weren't for some of us."

"I see."

Jim squirmed in his chair. "The trouble is that we've got to go over to Forest City tomorrow night," he said.

"Have you forgotten there's Bible club?"

"That's what bothers me, Danny. I know club is wonderful and all that, but they've asked us to help with the Cavalcade. They're counting on us." He took a deep breath. "They asked both Linda and me."

Danny Orlis folded his paper quite deliberately. "Have you told them you would be there, Jim?"

He nodded.

"I'm afraid Linda won't be able to go," Danny stated. "I've told her she had to stay in for the next two weeks."

Bible club on Thursday night was the smallest it had been since they started holding it. Four guys and a girl came a few minutes before eight. The girl sat down next to Linda and looked about curiously.

"Where is everybody?"

"They all went to Forest City to help get that Cavalcade set up."

"Sure wish they'd asked me on that deal. It sounds like it's going to be the great stuff," one of the boys put in.

"It beats this Bible study all to pieces," one of the other guys said. "I can tell you that much. I thought this was pretty good till we had the Cavalcade and I saw how exciting that was."

Linda Penner sighed wearily. "You can say that again. This is D-U-L-L Dull!"

Danny and Kay looked at one another helplessly.

* * *

On Friday morning Jim Morgan waited on the street corner and walked to school with Boyd Patterson.

"Say, Boyd," Jim said, "you really look bushed. What time did you get home last night?"

"Too late," he replied. "I thought I never was going to be able to get up this morning. And I've got to take an English test in the second period. Hope I don't go to sleep halfway through it."

"I thought you were going to take that test last night," Jim reminded him.

"I was supposed to, but I talked the teacher into letting me wait until the second period. Thought maybe I'd have a little more time to study." He yawned widely. "But the way things turned out I'd just as well have taken it yesterday. Didn't even get to crack a book."

Concern darkened Jim's youthful face. "I thought it would all be over by now. I tried to get to see you last night in Forest City, but someone was always talking. I've sure been praying for you."

Boyd nodded his appreciation. "Thanks. Believe me, I need it."

"Danny and Kay have been praying for you, too."

The boys entered school together.

"Guess I'd better run," Boyd Patterson called out. "I've got to have all the time I can get on this thing."

The English test Boyd had to take was a tough one. His heart sank when he read the questions.

Miss Kenyon's gaze sought his. "You had better

get to work, Boyd. The test is long and you don't have too much time."

He thought that when he finished she would correct it immediately, but she did not.

"I think I'll have time to correct your paper by Monday or Tuesday," she said. "I can let you know then."

"It sure would help if you could let me know today."

Her forehead crinkled. "What do you mean?"

"If I fail it again there wouldn't be much time for me to take it over before the Forest City game," he said, "unless you correct it right away."

"If you fail this test, Boyd, you won't be taking it over," she told him icily. "This is your last chance."

* * *

That afternoon when school was out Linda Penner left her homeroom and excitedly made her way down the corridor. Jack Ross had stopped her between classes an hour before and she hadn't been able to think of anything else since.

"You haven't got anything to do right after school, have you, Linda?" he asked.

"Not that I know of." She spoke breathlessly.

"Good. I want to see you."

And he had winked at her. He actually winked at her.

Linda's heart skipped a beat and her cheeks flushed with excitement. Jack had told her a week ago that he wanted to see her again, but she hadn't been sure whether he meant it or not. She didn't dare tell anyone. They would only have laughed at her. After all, she was just a ninth-grader and Jack would be a senior the next year.

A senior! And he really and truly wanted to go with her. Her heart sang. Just wait until the girls found out. They would be positively green with envy.

Linda stopped uncertainly and looked about. Jack had said he wanted to see her. Surely he wouldn't have been trying to make a joke of her. She was still there when Jim came by.

"Hi, Linda, looking for someone?"

"Oh, oh no. I–I just remembered I left something up in my locker."

"If you hurry you can ride with us," he told her. "We're going to distribute some more Cavalcade tickets."

"I–I wish I could, Jim, but I can't."

"I'll call Kay and see if I can fix it for you."

"That won't do any good."

"You've got to get busy and help with the Cavalcade, Linda. Know what's going to happen? The six kids who give out the most tickets get to ride over to Forest City in those slick Cad convertibles they use on the stage."

Linda's eyes widened. "That's dreamy."

"But there's only room for six!"

He went on down the corridor and out the front door of the school. Linda waited until he was gone before she left. She must have misunderstood Jack Ross. Maybe he meant that he wanted her to wait for him in the library or–

Her breath caught. There he was, sitting at the wheel of his car.

"Hi, Baby. I was about to give you up." He leaned over and opened the car door for her.

Color tinged her cheeks. "I–I'm sorry, Jack. I thought I was supposed to meet you inside." Fear clouded her eyes.

He laughed. "We'll let it go this time."

Jack started the engine and roared away with a start that left rubber on the pavement. "To tell you the truth I did plan on seeing you in school, but I figured Jim Morgan might be nosing around and I didn't want to get you in trouble."

Linda paused. "He was spying on me, but I got rid of him."

Jack whirled around the corner and sped toward the highway. "I got the little buggy tuned up like I said I would."

Her cheeks paled slightly. "I–I don't know whether I've got time to go very far, Jack." She spoke hesitantly.

"Don't you worry about that. I'll have you back to town before anyone misses you."

Jack Ross slowed for the stop sign, skidded around the corner, and as the car righted itself, jammed the accelerator to the floorboard. There was a deep, throaty roar.

Linda was slammed against the seat by the sudden burst of speed. "Jack!" The word escaped her lips involuntarily.

He laughed. "What's the matter, Baby?"

The speedometer needle touched seventy and continued to move upward. When at last Jack Ross pulled back into town Linda Penner was shaken and trembling.

"Well, what do you think of the old crate now?"

"I–I've never gone so fast in my whole life."

Jack nodded. "But just wait 'til I get my hands on enough money to soup the engine up the way it should be. Think maybe I can get 118 out of her."

Linda gasped.

"Did you like it?"

She managed a faint smile. "It–it was fabulous."

He broke into a broad grin again. "You're my kind of girl. Not afraid of anything."

He stopped at a corner a couple of blocks from the Orlis house and let her out. She was still trembling.

"Th-Th-Thanks, Jack."

"There are a couple of guys over in Forest City who really think they've got 'rods.' Beat me the last time we had a drag. But they won't beat me now. You and I'll go over and show 'em what our taillight and back bumper look like."

Linda said goodbye and walked hurriedly toward the house. Her heart was still beating frantically, and her face was moist with perspiration, but for all of that a strange thrill gripped her. Going riding with Jack was the most exciting thing she had ever done.

Shortly after she got home Jim Morgan came in. "Hi, Linda. Thought you were going to come straight home this afternoon."

She eyed him questioningly.

"I thought I saw you with Jack Ross a little while ago."

"He did take me home," she admitted.

"You weren't on the way home when I saw you. You were in the opposite end of town."

The color rushed back to her face and neck. "We did ride around for a little while, Jim. I was trying to talk him into going to Forest City to the Cavalcade." The lie came out easily.

"You'd better stay away from him. He's bad medicine."

She bristled. "What do you mean?"

"I'm givin' you the straight goods, Linda: there isn't a decent girl in high school who'll be seen with him."

"I'm not going to stand here and let you talk about my friends that way." She marched angrily out of the room.

* * *

Tuesday morning Jim walked to school with Boyd Patterson.

"Hear anything from that English test yet?"

Boyd nodded grimly. "I–I didn't make it. Miss Kenyon flunked me!"

Word that Boyd Patterson wasn't going to get

to pitch against Forest City spread rapidly over the school. Jim seemed to take it harder than anyone else.

"Now that Boyd isn't going to get to play, I don't think the game'll even be worth going to. We don't have a chance."

"Don't say that. Boyd isn't the whole squad."

"He's just about our whole squad. You know that as well as I do. Without him in there to pitch for us we can't beat anybody."

Linda Penner spoke up defiantly. "I don't know what's wrong with that Miss Kenyon. Why did she have to give Boyd a failing grade? Why didn't she pass him?"

"She would've passed him if he'd earned it," Danny said. "The trouble is that Boyd hasn't been studying the way he should have."

"That's right," Jim answered. "Even Boyd admits that Miss Kenyon gave him plenty of chances to get his work up. The trouble is he's been so busy with so many things he hasn't had time to study."

When they finished eating Linda Penner got to her feet and began to clear the table. Kay Orlis looked up at her in surprise.

"It's Jim's turn to do the dishes, Linda," she reminded her.

"I know." She smiled brightly but did not stop working. "I thought I'd help – if it's all right."

Jim Morgan spoke up quickly. "Sure, it's all right. In fact, it's just great."

"Which do you want to do, wash or dry?"

Jim's eyes narrowed suspiciously. "Are you sure you feel all right?"

When they were through with the dishes, Linda went to the living room door. "Is there something else you'd like to have me do, Kay?"

"I don't think so, Linda."

"I–I was wondering if I could go over to Mary's to study."

"You should be home by half-past nine."

Before leaving the house, she kissed Kay Orlis impulsively on the cheek.

"Now what brought all that on?" Danny asked.

"Perhaps Linda is beginning to respond to love, Danny, and to our prayers for her," Kay answered thoughtfully.

CHAPTER 11

THE COMPETITION IS HEAVY

Linda Penner left the Orlis house and walked hurriedly to the corner where Jack Ross was waiting in his car.

"You sure took your time, Kitten."

With a quick glance over her shoulder, she got into the car and scooted down into the seat. "I hurried as fast as I could."

Jack started the engine and drove away with a sudden burst of speed.

"I–I've got to be home by nine o'clock or a little later."

His voice raised, showing his disbelief. "You're joking."

"Isn't that positively nauseating?"

"You don't have to stand for that," Jack blustered. "Just tell 'em you're not goin' to be treated like a little kid. Tell 'em you've got some rights."

Linda was hesitant. "You don't know how they hate me, Jack. They'd like it fine if all I did was work around the house for them." She paused significantly.

"And to think, Daddy pays them so I can stay there and be their servant."

Jack Ross whipped the car around a tire-squealing corner. "Why don't you tell your dad?"

"He'd never believe anything about them." Her lips curled bitterly. "They go to *church*. They wouldn't do anything wrong."

Jack put his arm about her shoulder. "You poor kid. I'll try to make it up to you."

A few minutes later Jack turned on a side road and took out a cigarette. "Want one?"

She hesitated. "I–I don't think so."

He shrugged indifferently and lit his own.

"If I'd stayed out for baseball, I wouldn't be able to smoke."

Linda took a deep breath. "I sure wish Boyd were going to get to pitch against Forest City on Saturday."

Jack laughed. "It's his own fault he got kicked off the team."

"That's what Jim Morgan said. But I think it was terrible that Miss Kenyon had to flunk him."

"You couldn't expect anything more from an old witch like her." He finished his cigarette and flicked it out the window. "But Boyd didn't have to study and he didn't have to flunk, either. I had it all set up for him."

"What do you mean?"

"I'd taken that stupid test the day before and overheard her tell the principal she was going to give the same test to Boyd. I went right over to his house from school and told him about it. But do you know what he said?" Jack's voice rose in scorn. "He said he was a Christian and wouldn't even listen when I tried to tell him what the questions and answers were." Jack snorted. "All I can say is that it served him right."

For some reason a barb of guilt drove deeply into Linda Penner's heart. She shivered, although the evening was warm.

Another five minutes passed before either spoke.

"Jack," she began at last, "have you heard anything about the Christian Cavalcade that's to be held over at Forest City?"

He frowned thoughtfully. "There was something like that held here at Fairview, wasn't there? Isn't that some sort of a religious program?"

"Not exactly. What I mean is that it's the most exciting religious program you ever went to. They bring in the best singers and musicians you ever heard and have the most gorgeous costumes and everything."

"Hmm. Doesn't sound so bad."

"Bad? It's wonderful." Linda Penner turned to look at him appealingly. "Won't you go with me?"

He thought for a moment.

"If you would and Danny and Kay Orlis hear about it, things would be easier for–for *us*."

"I'll think about it."

Her heart sang.

Linda kept a close check on the time and a few minutes after nine she returned home. Danny, who was sitting at his desk in the living room, turned to survey her.

"I see you're back," he said warmly. "Have a good time?"

She frowned. "A good time studying?" she demanded.

"That's what had me wondering. You're so flushed and excited I thought you must have had a good time."

She did not answer him.

The night of the Christian Cavalcade in Forest City was also the regular night for Bible club. Danny and Jim talked about postponing it but decided not to.

"It's about the only night we can have club this week, Jim," Danny explained. "And some of the kids might be coming. I don't like to cancel club."

Jim Morgan nervously brushed his fingers through his hair. "Danny, would you and Kay feel awfully bad if I go to Forest City with the gang instead of coming to Bible club?"

"That's a decision you'll have to make," Danny told him.

"I'd like to be here for club, but I'm going to get to ride over to Forest City in one of those slick convertibles and–"

Linda Penner came in a little later. "Kay, I've got to talk to you about something," she began, her eyes sparkling with excitement.

"Yes." Kay stopped what she was doing and crossed

the kitchen to a chair. Linda sat down on the opposite side of the table.

"I told you I have a chance to ride to Forest City in one of those convertibles, but–but I've been talking to some of the kids about going to the Cavalcade and they want me to ride with them. That is, if it's all right with you and Danny."

Kay Orlis was silent for a moment. "We don't want you to go with a carload of kids, Linda," she reminded her. "There will have to be an adult along."

"Oh, I wouldn't want to go if there wasn't someone older to do the driving. One of the teachers is going with us."

* * *

Danny and Kay Orlis got ready for Bible club although they knew the attendance was going to be low. Jim Morgan and Linda Penner had already left for the Christian Cavalcade in Forest City.

"I don't know, Kay," Danny said. "Maybe we did make a mistake by not cancelling club tonight."

"This is a fine time to be talking that way. The kids will be coming any minute."

"If anyone does come," he said doubtfully. "The way I hear it, half the kids in town will be over at Forest City tonight."

At eight o'clock Boyd Patterson and a ninth-grade girl were the only ones who had arrived.

Danny Orlis grinned good-naturedly. "It looks as though the crowd's dropped off a little tonight. The competition's a little heavy."

"You can say that again," Boyd told him. "And I'm afraid I'd have been over to Forest City, too, if my parents hadn't grounded me for the duration of the school year. Guess they sort of blame the Cavalcade for the way my English grade slipped. Anyway, I can't go to anything except school events and Bible club."

Danny Orlis went through the motions of teaching the lesson, but it was obvious from the start that he wasn't getting it across. Even Boyd Patterson wasn't with him more than half the time, and when the lesson finally dragged to a close neither Boyd nor the girl stayed for lunch.

"I'd better get home," Boyd said lamely. "Maybe I can get in a little more studying before bedtime."

When they were gone Kay Orlis looked at her young husband helplessly. "Danny," she said miserably, "what are we going to do?"

He shook his head. "I sure don't know. It's a good thing they don't have this Cavalcade business every week. We can't compete with a production like that." He sighed wearily. "And, what's even worse, the kids are apt to get the idea that the Cavalcade actually represents Christianity. They don't realize that it's all frosting and no cake. So, good, solid teaching and Bible study soon get to be mighty dull stuff." Danny went over and switched off a floor lamp. "I know the promoters of this sort of thing mean well, but I'm afraid they're going to do a great deal of real harm."

* * *

Jim Morgan and Linda Penner left the house at about the same time that night, but they did not go to Forest City to the Christian Cavalcade together. Linda went down to the drugstore where she was to meet Jack Ross. He drove up twenty or thirty minutes late and sat out in front honking his horn.

"Oh, there's my date," she said to the girl she had been talking to, "I've got to run." With that she picked up her purse and hurried out to the car.

"Hi, Kitten," Jack greeted her, "hop in."

She opened the car door and got in beside him, speaking to the two couples in the back seat.

"I was beginning to think something had happened to keep you from coming, Jack," she said. "It's getting awfully late."

"Don't worry about a little thing like being late," he boasted. "When we get out on the highway so I can open up this old bus we'll make up for lost time."

One of the girls in the back giggled. "It's crowded back here," she said.

"That's just the way we want it, Baby," her boyfriend said.

All four of the kids in the back seat laughed loudly as Jack told a smutty joke. Linda Penner cringed.

"Think you'd dare open her up tonight?" one of the boys asked after a moment or two.

"Are you kiddin'?"

Jack Ross eased the car out on the highway and pushed the accelerator to the floorboard. The old car leaped ahead. One of the girls gasped.

Jack's laughter filled the car. "Just wait! You haven't seen anything yet."

Linda Penner saw the speedometer needle edge up to fifty-five, pass sixty-five and keep climbing. In spite of herself her agile young body stiffened with fear. "D-don't you think we're going awfully fast, Jack?" she managed.

"Fast?" he countered. "We're just gettin' warmed up. Just wait a sec and you'll really have something to talk about."

One of the guys in the back seat leaned forward. "Boy, this is great," he exclaimed. "How fast will she go, Jack?"

"Don't know yet. I've never got up nerve enough to open her up all the way."

The drive to Forest City was a nightmare. Linda Penner closed her eyes and prayed silently that Jack would slow down. But he did not. He wove the car expertly in and out of traffic, and jammed on the brakes only when it was absolutely necessary. The girls in the back screamed once or twice, but that only made him drive faster.

At last, they reached Forest City and he slowed down. "Now, where did you say we're going, Linda?" Jack asked.

"The Cavalcade is being held in the city auditorium," she told him.

Her heart was still pounding heavily when they got into the auditorium and sat down. The program was interesting enough. The entertainers were as good as they had been in Fairview. The talk at the close was just as challenging. But somehow it didn't seem that way to her. In a little more than an hour she would have to get back into the car with Jack and ride home.

The kids all seemed to enjoy the program, though. At least they seemed to enjoy it until the end, when the master of ceremonies gave his little talk which included the way of salvation, and made a long, impassioned altar call.

Even then, Jack Ross acted as though he was having a good time. He turned to one of his buddies and whispered hoarsely, "Go on, Tom. Go down front and get religion. That's just what you need, after what you were doing in the back seat coming over here."

The other boy sneered at him. "I don't need it any more than you do."

* * *

It was half an hour or more after the program was over that they pulled off the side road and started down the highway to Fairview. Linda Penner was sitting, white-lipped and trembling, on her own side of the seat, and anger glinted in Jack's eyes. He gripped the steering wheel tightly and jammed the accelerator to the floor.

Tom Graham started. "Hey," he exclaimed, "what're you doin'? We just want to go home. We don't want to go into orbit."

"Linda wants to get home!" Jack snapped. "So, I'm going to take her there! I might've known she'd be a wet blanket!"

He was still accelerating when one of the guys in the back seat cried out in warning.

"Radar trap!"

Almost at that very instant a patrol car whipped off the highway shoulder and started after them, siren whining.

CHAPTER 12

THE BUBBLES BURST

Fear drove the anger from Jack Ross's face. His knuckles showed white on the steering wheel and the powerful car surged forward. The kids in the car tensed.

"They've got to catch us first." He spat out the words.

Still the car behind them continued to close the gap. Linda grasped the seat with both hands and one of the girls in the back seat began to cry quietly.

Tom Graham touched Jack on the shoulder. "For cryin' out loud, Jack, use your head! Don't make it any worse than it is."

The driver's voice rose hysterically. "They're not goin' to get me and–and take my driver's license away from me! I can tell you that much!"

"You can't run away from that patrolman, no matter how fast you go," Tom told him. "He's drivin' a 'bomb.' And if you try to get away from <u>him,</u> he'll put us all in jail and throw away the key."

For a brief instant Jack Ross wavered in uncertainty. Then he lifted his foot from the accelerator. A minute or two later the patrolman pulled alongside and signaled for him to stop.

Sweat stood out on the young driver's face and forehead, and his hands were trembling on the steering wheel. Linda felt the muscles in her own throat contract fearfully. This would be in the paper for sure. What would she tell Danny and Kay then? How could she get out of this mess?

* * *

Danny and Kay Orlis were waiting up when Jim Morgan got home shortly after eleven. He opened the door and stuck his head in.

"Kay," he said, "do you suppose there's a chance for two starving boys to get something to eat?"

"I think so," she replied, "if they hurry."

Jim half turned to his companion. "Come on in, Don. I knew it would be all right. Kay's my buddy."

Lank, wiry Don Fleming, who had been at Bible club a few times, came into the kitchen with Jim and sat down at the table. Kay cut a cake she had baked that afternoon for Bible club and poured them tall glasses of ice-cold milk. About that time Danny Orlis came in to join them.

"Hi, guys," he greeted them, "did you have a good time?"

Jim nodded. "It was all right."

"All right?" Don echoed. "What's the matter with you, Jim? It was the greatest. You should've been there, Danny!"

Danny went over and got himself and Kay some milk.

Don Fleming continued to tell about the Cavalcade. "The crowd over there was a lot bigger than we had here by a long way, Danny," he said. "And you should've heard them clap. This one singer got three or four encores. I thought they never were going to let him quit."

Jim set his glass down and turned to Danny. "Have many kids out for club tonight?" he asked.

Danny shook his head. "As a matter of fact, it was real discouraging. We only had two. Boyd Patterson and a girl."

The boys finished their cake and Kay cut more for them. Don Fleming faced Danny.

"I liked Bible club all right," he said, "but I think it'd go over a lot better with the kids if you'd sort of 'jazz it up.'"

Danny's face wrinkled. "What?"

"You should 'jazz it up.' You know, pump some new life into it. Like I say, it's all right for some kids the way it is, but most of the crowd find it sort of dull. There'd be a lot bigger crowd if you gave them what they enjoy."

"We're having the same kind of meetings we used to have when you kids were filling the living room every Thursday night," Danny reminded him. "That's the thing that makes this all seem so strange to me."

"You had kids coming out for Bible club," Don admitted, "but you should see how they come out for these Cavalcades. We were all talking about it in the car coming home. If we could have a good program every week, I'll bet it wouldn't be long until we wouldn't be able to pack all the kids into the living room. Why, I'll bet we'd have to meet down at the Municipal Building or somewhere else where we'd have space enough to get all the kids in."

Jim Morgan set his milk on the table and laid aside his cake. "You know, Danny," he said deliberately, "I've really been sold on this Cavalcade, and I'll have to confess that I used to think you were stuffy and old-fashioned for feeling the way you do about it."

Danny's gaze met his, questioningly, but he did not reply.

"But I've changed my mind," he continued.

"You have? When did that happen?"

"I guess it started when we were having the program tonight," Jim said, "but listening to the gang talk about it afterwards made me see that there's something wrong. We can't win people to Christ and get them really established in their faith by putting on entertainment for them like the world does."

Don Fleming was skeptical and defensive. "What do you mean? I thought you liked it."

"I guess I had a good time while I was there, Don. But I didn't feel any closer to God because I went. I didn't learn more about surrendering or living for

Him. There were some unsaved kids in our car coming home. They didn't act as though they were under conviction, either. The things they said were just glorifying some Christian entertainers. Isn't that right?"

Don was slow in answering. "Well–"

"I can see now that Bible club and memorizing Scripture and taking part in the activities of the church and witnessing are the things that are going to help us learn more about Christ and living for Him. Those are the things that are going to get us established in our faith. These frothy things aren't going to help much."

Danny nodded. "You've got a point there, Jim, and I'm sure glad to see that you came to that decision on your own. It doesn't do much good to have contact with a lot of kids if you don't use that opportunity to give them something worthwhile." He took a deep breath. "Of course, we've got to be careful that we don't criticize all Christian musicians. We've had a good many wonderful programs in our church which were musical and still Christ was edified. I think it's the way the thing is done more than what is done, that I find objectionable."

There was a long silence.

Finally, Don Fleming looked at his watch. "It's getting late. I've got to run!"

When he was gone Kay noted the time. "Linda should have been home long before now."

Jim snorted. "You'd just as well forget about waiting up for her," he told them. "That crowd she's with think the evening's just getting started at midnight."

Concern gleamed in Kay's eyes. "One of the teachers went along, didn't he?"

"You wouldn't catch Jack Ross having a teacher along if he could help it. That'd cramp his style." Jim was looking from one to the other. "I–I didn't mean to squeal on Linda," he said lamely.

Danny Orlis' face was stern. "I think you'd better start at the beginning, Jim, and tell Kay and me all about this boy Linda is with tonight."

Jim Morgan spoke reluctantly. "Well, if I had a sister," he said, "Jack Ross is sure not the kind of a guy I'd be wanting her to go with. That's for sure."

They were still talking when Linda Penner came into the house. Fright still marked her young face.

"Are you still up?" she asked, making a strained attempt at gaiety. "I thought you'd all be in bed a long time ago."

"I think you have some explaining to do, Linda," Danny said sternly. "You didn't tell us the truth. There was no teacher with you."

The dark-haired girl whirled angrily and glared at Jim Morgan. "I–I was going to tell you about it. I knew Jim would come home and–and tattle on me."

"Jim let something slip," Danny corrected her, "and I insisted that he tell me the rest."

Linda managed to look him straight in the eye with a gaze that did not waver. "I thought one of the teachers was going to be along," she said. "Honestly, I did. And so did Jack. But at the last minute he got a–a headache and wasn't able to go." She paused momentarily, as though to see whether her story was believed or not. "I–I suppose I should've called and told you about it, but I was so anxious to have the kids who were going with us hear the Gospel that–that all I could think of was getting them to Forest City." An appealing note came into her voice. "I–I'm sorry, Danny," she said. "I won't do it again."

Danny Orlis was unmoved. "We'll finish talking about this tomorrow after I call the school and talk with the teacher who was supposed to go with you."

The fear leaped back into Linda's dark eyes. "You–you mean you don't trust me?"

"Should I?"

Tears welled in her eyes and trickled down her cheeks. "You won't believe me when I do tell you the truth."

"Now stop that crying, Linda," Danny ordered. "I've got to talk to you."

She stifled her sobbing and wiped at her eyes in silence.

"Trust is something that has to be earned," he continued. "I wouldn't be fair to you. I wouldn't be discharging my responsibility to your father if I didn't insist on proof that you are telling me the truth under circumstances like this." He took a deep breath. "You don't realize it, Linda, but your whole future is at stake. If we allow you to go on you will likely get into serious trouble."

Linda Penner fought to control her trembling lips. "I–I was afraid you wouldn't let me go with Jack and the kids if–if you knew no adult was going to be along. But I–I learned my lesson."

She burst into tears, and before either Danny or Kay could speak, she had fled to her room. In a moment or two Kay Orlis followed her. Linda was lying on the bed, her shoulders shaking.

Kay sat down beside her. "You're not just crying about the story you told us that isn't true, are you?" she asked.

Linda sat up. "How did you know?"

"That look on your face told me."

The girl began to sob again, quietly. "I'll–I'll never trust another guy again. If boys are like that, I'm not even going to have another date!"

Kay Orlis put an arm about Linda's shoulder, tenderly, and held her close. "Would you like to tell me about it?" she asked.

Haltingly Linda related the story of how Jack Ross had insisted on parking on a lonely side road after the Cavalcade, and how angry he had become when she wouldn't act the way the other two girls in the car were acting.

Linda's voice broke again. "That was when Jack started driving like crazy and–and was arrested and everything. Now, he says that it was all my fault."

Kay Orlis spoke to her gently. "Linda, this is the reason your daddy and Danny and I don't want you to date yet. And this is why we want you to be so careful about who you go with and whether or not the boys are older than you are, when you do start to date."

I–I don't think I'm ever going to want to go on another date again," she blurted.

"Oh, yes, you will," Kay told her quietly. "And when you're old enough you should go with boys. It's part of growing up. This whole business of dating is serious. Far too many boys don't know how to treat girls with respect and consideration, and far too many girls are so concerned about being popular, that they don't keep their standards high."

Kay stayed in the bedroom with Linda for more than an hour. When she came out, Danny was nodding sleepily in a chair. He looked up.

"That must've been some conversation. Were you able to get anywhere with her? Did you get a chance to deal with her spiritually?"

There was a moment's silence. "Linda protests that she does know Christ as her Savior, Danny," Kay replied. "I'm not at all sure that she does, but I know this much. The things that happened tonight were just enough to show her where she is headed if she keeps on rejecting Christ….

"We can thank God for that."

Before getting into bed, they knelt together to pray for the girl who was staying with them, that she might take Christ as her Savior. When they finished Kay's eyes were shining.

"I don't know when or how it's going to happen," she said softly, "but I have complete assurance that one day she will take the Lord Jesus Christ as her personal Savior."

THE DANNY ORLIS SERIES

The Danny Orlis series, by Bernard Palmer, delivers a blend of adventure, mystery, and suspense through various settings—from the Canadian wilderness to Guatemalan jungles. Danny Orlis, an adept outdoorsman, skilled athlete, and committed Christian, employs his quick thinking, calm bravery, and biblical solutions to confront everyday problems and hair-raising dangers. Early stories focus on Danny navigating school life, sports, and outdoor challenges, while in later books, Danny and his wife Kay provide wisdom and guidance to youngsters facing lifelike situations and challenges. Having sold over two million copies, this series has made Palmer a renowned author in Christian youth literature. Palmer is also the author of the Felicia Cartright series and various other series for Christian youth.

AVAILABLE FROM WWW.ANEKOPRESS.COM

www.ingramcontent.com/pod-product-compliance
Lightning Source LLC
Chambersburg PA
CBHW070703010826
48975CB00015B/2621